SURPRISED AND SACKED

KNOXVILLE COYOTES FOOTBALL
BOOK 2

GINA AZZI

THREE CITIES PUBLISHING LLC

1

WEST

The stadium erupts—I'm talking, ear-splitting, raucous, incredulous joy—as my teammate, wide receiver Cohen Campbell dances in the end zone.

Holy shit. The slight bite of an evening chill hits me in the face as disbelief swims through my veins, and I freeze. We won the Super Bowl!

I repeat: The Knoxville Coyotes just won the motherfucking Super Bowl.

Elation like I've never known rushes through my body. I pull off my helmet and spin around slowly, gazing up at the stands, taking in the cheering fans, the swarm of crimson and gold jerseys, the *moment*.

This moment.

The green turf of the football field fans around me, an endless stretch, as if I'm standing in the center of the universe. For a heartbeat, a blink, a second, pure gratitude overwhelms the adrenaline pumping in my veins.

I've trained for this. Prayed for it. Dreamed it up countless times.

So many nights staring at a flaking, popcorn ceiling, listening to the fighting ring out below, I imagined *this*.

And still, the moment is sweeter than anything I hoped for.

"Way to go, boy!" Jag Baglione jumps on my back, slapping my shoulder.

"One hell of a game, you fucking rookie!" Gage Gutierrez agrees, punching my arm before pulling me into a side hug.

A wide smile cuts my face as I grin in shock.

"We won the Super Bowl," I mutter. A Super Bowl I played in. Hell, started in. Fuck, scored a touchdown in.

"Yeah, we did!" Our team captain, Avery Callaway whoops.

The team rushes then, all of us surrounding Callaway as friends and family begin to pour onto the field.

Our huddle buzzes with energy. A shared pulse as we wrap our arms around each other. Our bodies sway in unison, tapping from one foot to the next, bouncing, with collective inhales and exhales rounded out with excitement.

"Coyotes!" we yell, slapping each other's backs before stepping back to accept the congratulations from our loved ones.

The excitement of my teammates vibrates off their frames, causing the air to expand, and a wave of incredulity to sweep us all.

Flashes go off, momentarily blinding me.

Coaches Strauss and Stevens hug us tightly.

Confetti falls from above like snow, dousing us in crimson and gold sparkles.

I drag in a breath, my hands closing into fists.

I am living my dream. The dream. The ultimate goal.

And she's not here to see it.

Disappointment blooms in the pit of my stomach, erupting upwards until it clogs my throat.

I shake my head, dispelling the thought. I clear my throat, dislodging the emotion.

Nova and I called it quits at the start of the season. I

haven't spoken to her in months. She's not part of my life right now and the fact that I still conjure her up during my highest highs and lowest lows should infuriate me.

Instead, I miss her.

"You've got one hell of a career ahead of you, son," Coach Strauss mutters, smacking my back. "Go enjoy your win." He shoves me toward the locker rooms where the team is relocating.

While media outlets vie for our attention and a few of the guys get pulled into interviews, I steer clear. I'm not great at giving interviews. The PR team says I need to share more of my feelings and sentiments about the team rather than sticking to the technical aspects of the game. Be more relatable. But, hell, I'm not great at forging personal connections.

Not the meaningful kind anyway.

Except for her....

Stop it!

I step toward Avery and Cohen when a glimpse of familiarity slows my steps.

Derek Reiner, from The Burnt Clovers, and his girlfriend Allegra Rousell. Derek's got A tucked under his arm. Allegra, who is Nova's best friend, laughs at something Derek says and then, she turns.

Color drains from my face.

My heart drops to my feet. And stays there.

My breath fucking freezes in my lungs.

She's right there. She's fucking here.

Nova Jeanne Martin.

Her blonde hair is pulled away from her face in a low, sleek ponytail. Her petite frame is decked out fashionably—especially for a football game. Designer black jeans hug her hips and wrap around her slender calves. She's wearing trendy black boots—with a heel—since she hates being shorter than everyone else.

I smirk when I note that underneath her gold puffer vest,

she's wearing a Coyotes jersey. My jersey. Number 31. That's right. Nova better have my name across her back.

Jesus. I shake my head. I can't believe she's here.

I study her and the noise of the stadium—thunderous seconds ago—ceases to exist. Instead, I'm pulled into Nova's orbit. How can I not be when she's my real-life supernova? Too bright to last too long. Is that why we burned out?

As if she can feel my stare, Nova looks up and her eyes—a soft brown ringed with sage—latch onto mine.

She sucks in a sharp inhale, her hand lifting to press against the center of her chest.

My hands curl into fists as I'm hit with the first wave of her recognition. Christ, it threatens to pull me under.

How have I lasted this long with no connection to her? Without hearing her musical laughter or noting how she wrinkles her nose when she's unsure. Without the reassuring touch of her hand linked around the crook of my elbow. God, I've missed her.

Allegra notes our exchange and threads her arm with Nova's, beelining toward me as my teammates, and their friends and families, continue to celebrate around us.

"Congratulations, West," Allegra says, grinning at me.

I manage a smile. "Thanks, A."

"You were fucking fire!" Derek announces, slapping me on the back.

"Hey, man." I give him a side hug. "Thanks for coming."

"Wouldn't miss this," he replies.

I lift an eyebrow. Derek Reiner is an internationally cele-brated rockstar. While he's invited to all major sporting events, he doesn't regularly attend them.

He ducks his head sheepishly. "Levi's speaking at a rehab facility that one of his sponsors started through the Harrison Foundation."

"Sweet," I laugh. "So, you were already in town?"

"Yeah," he agrees, tucking Allegra back under his arm.

His eyes dart to Nova before settling back on mine. "We'll give you guys a minute."

"Thanks," I say, meaning it. But I'm going to need more than a minute with Nova.

Hell, I'd take eternity if I could. But since that's not meant to be, I need to lay this shit between us to rest. Once and for all.

I need to move on.

My chest pinches at the thought.

Allegra bites her bottom lip but before she can add to the conversation, Derek drags her away. I stifle a chuckle, appreciating his help in giving me face time with my girl.

Except, she's not mine anymore.

"I didn't know you were coming," I murmur.

Nova shrugs and moves to tuck her hair behind her ears, the way she does when she's nervous. Since it's already pulled back, her fingertips brush over the shells of her ears and she sighs. "It was a last-minute thing."

"How's your dad?" I ask. That was the first strike against us. Not because her father didn't like me, but because his heart attack last August meant Nova's permanent return to Paris. What was supposed to be a quick visit turned into weeks and then, months.

I didn't think the long-distance would be so hard for us. Turns out, it was the kiss of death.

"He's okay," she says softly. "This is my first time away since…"

Since she left. Over five months ago.

"I'm glad you're here," I admit, meaning it.

She smiles at me, but her eyes are sad. "I couldn't miss this. You were…" She shuffles closer. "West, you were incredible out there. I'm so proud of you."

Her words, laced with the pride she freely shares, causes my throat to tighten.

"Thank you," I whisper.

She's the only person truly here for me. Sure, there are some college buddies in the stands who are rooting for me. There are friends of friends and high school acquaintances who got last-minute tickets. Even one of my old coaches came to show his support which means a lot to me, especially since my high school coach—Coach Kent—who was more of a father to me than any other man, passed away years ago.

But the solid, familial support that most of my teammates know and rely on doesn't exist for me. I've only ever had Nova. And then, not even that.

The fact that she's here causes the emotions I keep at bay to rise to the surface and flood my system.

Nova smiles again, her face lighting up. Christ, she's beautiful. "You did it, West. All your dreams came true."

Not all of them.

I swallow back the words.

Force a fucking grin.

"Yeah," I agree. "How long are you in town for?"

She drops one shoulder in a half shrug. "Just the weekend. Dad and my brothers need me back. I'm starting a tasting room for the label in Paris and I'm already renovating the space."

I smile for real this time. "That's incredible, Nova. Your dad's lucky to have his legacy in great hands."

She chuckles. "I don't know about that." She sighs. "It isn't the fashion career I dreamed of, but right now, it's good. It's nice to be by family again."

"Yeah," I say. I wonder what that feels like. I'll never know. "Well, you should come to the after-party." I tilt my head and stare at her. Now that she's here, I don't want to miss a second.

We never got closure. Our breakup wasn't dramatic. It was a slow growing apart of two people who respect each other. We had jobs to do, commitments to uphold. And we couldn't balance us amid them.

As the weeks went by, we became less like lovers and more like friends. Then, acquaintances. Now, practically strangers.

But my feelings for her, they're just as intense and meaningful as when we laid in the bed of my truck, looked up at the night sky, and whispered our dreams into the darkness.

I want to be a fashion designer, she admitted.

I want to win a Super Bowl, I confessed.

"I don't know," Nova hesitates. She rocks from one foot to the next.

"Please, Nova. Come," I state.

One last night with you and then I'll let you go. I'll move on, I bargain with the universe.

Give me tonight and I'll stop asking for a second shot.

She stares at me for a long moment. Emotions I can't read filter through her eyes. Then, she nods. "All right, West. One last night."

"One last hurrah." I grin. "I wouldn't want to celebrate tonight with anyone else."

A streak of pride blazes across her expression before she dips her head in acknowledgment. She swats at me playfully. "Go shower. I'll wait for you." She looks down at her clothes. "Actually, I need to change. I'll—"

"You look perfect, Nov."

She smirks. "Pick me up on your way to the party?"

"You brought a fancy dress for a party you didn't know you'd be attending?" I joke.

"I knew you'd win tonight."

"You didn't tell me you were coming."

Nova wrinkles her nose. "I was half hoping I'd see you."

I cross my arms over my chest. "And the other half?"

She lets out a long exhale. "Terrified."

"Why?" I whisper as fear and hope mix in my gut.

"Because we'll never have more than this," she admits,

gesturing between us. "And it will never be enough." She closes the space between us and lifts up onto her tippy toes.

I bow down as she presses her lips to my cheek. "I'll text you the address, West. Pick me up."

"I'll be there," I promise.

Then I watch as my girl, the only one who has ever owned my heart, walks away.

Fuck, I miss her.

It guts me that I'll never have her.

All we'll have is tonight.

A celebration.

And closure.

"You're coming," I say, turning to check out the back of my dress in the hotel's mirror.

Allegra doesn't reply and I cut my gaze to hers in the reflection.

She smirks. "As if I'd let you go solo."

Relief flows through me and I smile at A. "Thank you."

"What was it like, seeing him again?"

I face the mirror and pretend to fix my lip liner as I choose my words. "Everything," I admit. "I miss him. I miss him so much. And yet"—I turn to look at Allegra—"I'm proud of him." I grin. "He won! I mean, that was his biggest dream, and he did it his first season as a rookie!"

"He had an incredible season," she agrees.

"Didn't know you were keeping tabs." I raise an eyebrow.

Derek snorts as he enters my hotel room. We're staying in a three-bedroom suite—me, Derek and Allegra, and Allegra's brother Levi who skipped the game to catch up with one of his sponsors from rehab. That's why Derek, Allegra, and Levi are in town—to show support for a new clinic Levi's sponsor is opening through a partnership with the Harrison Foundation.

When Allegra called me about the Super Bowl tickets, I

didn't think. I just packed, booked a flight, and made it to Knoxville as quickly as I could. It wasn't rational. In fact, if I think it over logically, it was stupid.

This visit threatens to set back all the progress I've made over the past five months. Moving on from West has been debilitating. But necessary. Seeing him tonight has already affected me. Spending the next few hours talking to him? Laughing with him? Feeling his strength envelop me as he wraps an arm around my waist? I don't stand a fucking chance.

A masochist. That's what I am.

Or just foolishly in love with a man I can't have.

"What?" I ask the infamous rockstar.

"Of course, we kept tabs. To be honest, it wasn't hard. West is the best rookie—and one of the most talked about running backs—in the league."

"Facts. And," Allegra continues, pointing at me. "I know you aren't over him."

Derek's mouth twitches but he doesn't say anything. I stick my tongue out at him, and he shakes his head, bends to place a quick peck on Allegra's lips, and leaves the room. "I'm ready when you are!" he calls over his shoulder.

"You're not," Allegra repeats, looking at me, as if Derek didn't waltz in here to check on girl talk. He pretends he's not invested but he wants the spilled tea as much as any of us.

I sigh. "Of course, I'm not. I don't know if I'll ever be over West, but I have to move on. I can't keep wondering what he's up to or what's happening in his life. Not when he's here, I'm in Paris, and my family needs me. Dad and my brothers entrusted me with a huge project. They've given me a lot of leeway to try new things, to find my footing within the family business. I don't want to let them down."

Allegra's expression softens. "You won't, Nova." She stands and walks toward me. She spins me until we're both facing the mirror. Then, she slings an arm around my waist and tips her head against mine. "You never let anyone down."

"Except West," I admit. I can still hear the heartache laced in his voice when we ended things for good. It was a phone call, a broken goodbye, a string of text messages that gathered more time in between replies.

And then, it was over.

"Enjoy tonight," Allegra gives me a squeeze. "You look fierce."

I manage a small smile as I drag my palms over my hips. I'm wearing a short, gold body con dress with thin straps. My hair is still pulled back, so I paired it with crimson-red drop earrings.

"One last hurrah," I murmur, repeating West's words.

Then, I slip into a leather jacket, slide into my pumps, and tuck a clutch under my arm.

Tonight, I'm going to enjoy my time with West. Because in the morning, it will all be over. Done. For real this time.

Allegra and Derek promise to meet us at the after-party. As such, I slide into the passenger seat of West's ride solo, and I'm met with a slew of memories.

Riding shotgun, with my feet stacked on his dashboard, singing out of tune to oldies music.

Making out every time a simple good-night kiss turned into so much more.

Laying in the bed of his truck and staring up at the stars, making wishes, sharing dreams.

I click in my seat belt, pull in a breath, and savor it.

"I figured you'd buy a new ride," I joke, leaning back into the comfortable, well-worn leather of his F-150.

West smirks. "Nah. Too many memories with Tillie."

I snort, shaking my head at his truck's name.

But Tillie's been a part of our story since the beginning, and I love that he held onto his truck. Onto the memories we made in her.

"You look stunning, Nov." West's eyes burn as he glances at me. One side of his mouth pulls into a smile. "Too pretty to be on my arm."

"Shut up," I joke, swatting at him.

He slips his palm over the top of the steering wheel and pulls away from the Premier Hotel.

"What've you been up to?" West asks after a few seconds of silence.

I study his profile as he drives. His hair is cropped close to his head, but the top showcases his brown curls. I used to love twirling them around my finger and tugging to get his attention. West is freshly shaved, his jawline stronger than I remember. High cheekbones, a cleft in the center of his chin, and a dimple that appears in his right cheek when he smiles.

God, I've missed him.

"Nov?" He glances at me. His eyes are so dark, they're nearly black.

I clear my throat. Flash a smile. "Working mostly. My first few months were spent taking care of Dad. He's stable now and in good spirits. But he's not able to work the way he used to. It was a lot for my brothers, so they've turned a good chunk of it—first, the tasting rooms, and now, several accounts too—over to me. I really want to finalize the tasting space in Paris. Gabriel and Jacques are used to doing every-thing from the vineyard, but I think having a presence in the city will make a big impact. Especially with the restaurants we're trying to woo."

"Wow," West says, nodding along. "You've been busy, babe." The term of endearment slips from his mouth and neither of us corrects it.

Babe. Yeah, it's a generic word.

But when West says it…butterflies dance in my belly, their wings turning my nerves into excitement. *Expectation.*

"Yeah," I agree. "Well, you've been unstoppable. How do you like Knoxville?"

West tilts his head, considering my question. "I like it. I mean, the team's incredible. Facilities are top-notch. Coaches are great. It just…you know, it takes me time to find my place is all."

"Yeah." West keeps to himself until he connects with someone. Until that point, he's friendly and loyal but doesn't give himself fully. It took months for me to wear him down, and even after we exchanged declarations of love, he never shared all the details of his painful childhood or how much his mother's death affects him. "I remember," I say lightly.

He chuckles and reaches over, placing a hand on my thigh. He gives it a gentle squeeze and a shiver runs down my spine.

It feels so natural. So…*right.*

And yet, this is it. I need to stop living in the past and move…forward. Focus on Paris. On my family. The business.

"Please," West scoffs. "Took me no time where you were concerned."

And I know that from his perspective—and how few people he's counted on in his life—he's telling the truth. West let me in deeper than anyone else and now, we're both trying to heal from the heartache our breakup caused.

Still, his words light me up from the inside out. The truth is, we fell for each other fast. Hard. And it was easy. *Right.*

I shake my head. "I wish our circumstances were different."

He gives me a look. Those eyes midnight black and solemn as hell. "Me too, baby. More than you know."

A beat of silence passes and then, I reach for the volume, turning it up to lighten the mood. "All right, West. Tonight, we celebrate your success. You won! And I'm here to witness it. Tonight's a good night."

He nods slowly. When he looks at me again, there's more warmth in his gaze. "Tonight's a great night, Supernova."

I snort at the stupid nickname. It's hardly original, but again, when West says it, it holds a different meaning.

He pulls in front of a downtown club. Getting out of his truck, he tosses his keys to a valet. When the guy notes West, he scrambles forward.

"West Crawford!" the valet exclaims, jutting out a hand. "It's an honor to meet you."

"Thanks, man! Keep my baby Tillie safe, yeah?" West asks.

The kid's eyes are round as teacup saucers. "Of course."

West chuckles. Easy. Affable. So goddamn likable. I wonder if people realize how much more depth there is to him. He always said I was the only person who truly knows him.

And eventually, someone else will too, right? Another woman. Ugh. The thought sours my stomach.

Stop it. Tonight is a good night. A celebration.

"Appreciate you." West points at the valet as he rounds the front of the truck.

Then, he's pulling open the passenger door. Extending his hand, like a gentleman. Staring at me with so many emotions in his eyes, it makes my head spin.

"You ready, Nov?"

I nod and step down from his truck. Even in heels, the top of my head barely grazes his chin. "Ready."

He laces our fingers together and leads me into an after-party that is both elegant and wild. Glitzy and raucous.

A cheer rings out when West crosses the threshold.

I note the surprise in his teammates' gazes, the hate on the faces of women who are always going to hate, and the curious glances of everyone else, as they clock my hand in his.

But I ignore everyone because I'm here for West.

And yeah, it may not be for forever. But for tonight, he's my sole focus. I don't care about photographers and social media posts. I'm not interested in gossip and rumors.

I'm here because I couldn't not show up for the man who showed me what being in love feels like.

It's bittersweet as hell but for tonight, I get to drown in the sweet and save the bitter for another day. Like tomorrow.

"You made it!" the team captain, Avery, says, passing us each a flute of champagne.

"Yeah," West mumbles, never good at small talk.

"Congratulations!" I drop West's hand to accept the flute and hold out my free hand toward Avery. "I'm Nova."

A flicker of recognition zips through his irises.

Does the team know about me? What did West tell them? We were together through training camp and preseason but were hardly speaking by the time the regular season was underway.

"Good to meet you," Avery says neutrally.

I dip my head. I like that he gives nothing away. I like that he has West's back. West deserves teammates that protect him. God knows he spent years of his life protecting others.

"Hi!" a friendly voice rings out. In the next moment, a woman who bears a resemblance to Avery appears. "I'm Raia! I'm this one's sister." She pushes Avery's shoulder. "And that one's girlfriend." She points to a blond guy who is making a group of people crack up as he juggles bottles of tequila.

I grin and give a little wave. "Nice to meet you, Raia. I'm Nova."

"Come on, come meet everyone." Raia latches onto my arm and pulls me deeper into a VIP area where the team is hanging out.

I glance at West, but he gives me a nod, letting me know I'm in good hands. His team captain leans closer and mutters something to him.

West looks away and I suck in an inhale.

Tonight, I need to walk a fine line. I may have arrived on West's arm but when I leave tonight, I'm doing it solo.

No looks back.

No second chance.

There's only this moment. And then, I have to say goodbye.

Lifting the champagne flute to my lips, I take a sip.

The bubbles dance over my tongue and down my throat. I relish the crisp sweetness and steel my shoulders.

Tonight, I'm here to celebrate West Crawford.

3

WEST

"That your ex?" Avery asks as Nova disappears into what could be a team huddle.

"Kind of."

Avery lifts a skeptical eyebrow. "And she just showed up tonight?"

"It's not what you think, man."

"Really?" His tone is understanding but his eyes are hard.

I know he's just looking out and I appreciate that but, "Really." My tone is firm. "Nova and I didn't have a messy, complicated breakup. Her family needed her in France, so she showed up for them. I made a commitment here, and I followed through. There's no future for us but there's mad respect." I shake my head. "It's all good."

Avery nods, his gaze narrowed on the back of Nova's head. "If you say so, Crawford."

"I do." I shut the conversation down.

Avery sighs. "Go get a real drink." He plucks the champagne flute from my hand. "I know you can't stand this bubbly crap."

"Thanks, Cap." I slap his shoulder.

Then, I walk into the VIP area, exchange congratulations

with my teammates, sink onto a sofa next to my girl, and toss back a vodka and soda.

Music plays and groups of women dance, vying for our attention. But my focus is trained on Nova. I love that she listens attentively as Jag explains the design for his Super Bowl ring. She nods enthusiastically and asks questions when Cohen brags about Raia's signing to play soccer for the Chicago Tornados. She fits into my life—a life I struggle to embrace—effortlessly. Like months haven't passed without us speaking. Like I'm not half heartbroken, desperately hoping our circumstances were different.

When I rented a place in Knoxville, I thought about how she would decorate it. When my teammates poked fun at my ride, I realized I couldn't sell Tillie because of the memories I made with Nova in my old truck. For months, she's been a phantom presence in my life.

And now, she's here, and I wonder how I'll get over her again.

But, fuck, I have to.

I accept a shot of tequila from Gage and toss it back with my teammates.

As the alcohol works its way through my system, I relax. Let my guard down. Grin when Derek shows up with A. Laugh as Nova drags me out onto the dance floor. Swear when she presses her tight-ass body up against my frame and begins to grind.

My hands find her hips and rest there. As she pushes back against me, I drop my chin to her shoulder. "You dance with other men like this?" The question pops out of my mouth as a flare of jealousy pierces my mind at the thought. I'd want to break the fingers of any guy who put his hands on Nova.

Fuck, I've got no right to ask it. But hell if I don't want to know.

Has she been with another man since we parted ways?

The thought is fucking painful. Devastatingly so.

My girl spins in my arms and tucks her hand in the back pocket of my slacks. "Just you, West." And I believe her.

I relax a little bit more. Accept another shot glass of tequila from Talon Miller.

I clink the glass against Nova's. A few drops spill over the rim and land on her wrist. Taking her hand in mine, I bring it to my lips and kiss the drops, my tongue darting out to lick the tequila straight from her skin.

She sucks in a breath, her eyes locked on mine.

"What are we toasting to?" Nova asks, waving her shot glass.

"Your future," I say, sounding less bitter than I feel.

She shakes her head. "Your success."

"Is that what this is?" I ask, glancing around the massive party. I mean, obviously, it is. But without Nova permanently in my life, everything feels a little emptier, duller, than it's supposed to.

"West," she chides, pain in her voice.

I clear my throat. Damn, I don't want to fuck this up. Waste it.

Not when I should be savoring these seconds.

"I'm sorry, baby." I mean it.

"I know." She takes my hand and squeezes my fingers. "To beautiful pasts and bright futures." She lifts her glass again.

I squeeze her hand back twice, just the way I used to. Then, I tap my shot glass against hers, down it in one gulp, and close my eyes.

I breathe in the scent of Nova—light and airy. Floral and fleeting.

I clock the feel of her hand on my hip.

I wrap an arm around her back and hold her close. Enjoy the moment.

Then, I vow to savor the night. To be present with Nova

for however many hours we have. And to let her go tomorrow.

When I open my eyes and glance down, she's staring at me. Her irises are flecked with gold, made more apparent from the color of her dress.

"I miss you," I admit.

"Me too," she agrees.

Then, I lower my mouth to hers and kiss her. Claim her. And give her up all in the same heartbeat.

Except she slants her head, dips her tongue into my mouth, and gives me a piece of herself.

And fuck if I don't take it all.

The rest of the night passes in flashes and blurs. Raia, Nova, and Allegra join some other women I don't recognize for a dance battle. It's fucking hilarious and Cohen has tears streaming down his cheeks as he films the girls trying to one-up each other with throwback dance moves.

Tequila shots arrive on trays and quickly disappear.

Derek finally caves to the constant begging and belts out two lines from The Burnt Clovers' hit song, "That Summer."

Nova's face is flushed, her cheeks red with excitement, her eyes bright with joy. She looks just how I remember and, for a second, I'm terrified that one day I'll forget.

The next time she passes me, I reach out and wrap an arm around her waist. "You've got moves, Nova Jeanne."

She smirks, turning in my arms to place her hands on my chest. "You've seen most of them, Crawford."

"But not all?"

She bites her bottom lip and slowly shakes her head. "I've got one or two I can bust out."

I snort, a bark of laughter spilling from my mouth.

A few of my teammates give me a strange look.

Nova catches the exchange and when her eyes meet mine, there's a sadness in their depths. "They don't hear you laugh often?"

"No one hears me laugh as much as you," I say honestly.

She exhales slowly. The top of her head barely grazes my chin and still, we fit together perfectly. We line up in all the ways that matter most. "Do you have plans tonight? Afterward?" Her voice is hesitant.

I roll my lips together to keep from smiling. "Only if they include you."

She grins. "They better include me."

"I'd hope so. I wanna see you bust out one of these moves you're bragging about."

Nova laughs and gives me a coy look. "Oh, I'll teach you a thing or two, Crawford."

"I'm counting on it." I tap her ass lightly. "Go, dance. I like watching you have fun."

"I always have the most fun with you," she promises, leaning up to kiss my cheek. "Tonight, West."

"Tonight," I confirm.

Then, I watch Nova light up the room, make friends with a genuine smile and easy small talk. I stare at her and realize, fully, what could have been.

What should have been.

And what will never be.

4

Nova

I'M BREATHLESS WHEN WE STUMBLE INTO WEST'S CONDO.

"You have a view of the city," I murmur, my eyes cutting to the floor-to-ceiling windows behind him.

"It's a good spot," he murmurs, his lips pressed against my neck. "Centrally located."

I giggle and nod in agreement. His condo is one street away from the club, allowing us to leave his truck and the party behind. It was easy to sneak away to steal these hours for us.

I hear the condo door close behind me and sink further into West's hold. "I should message Allegra."

"Derek saw us leave," West explains, his fingers pulling down the zipper of my dress. When he reaches the end of the zipper, his palm slides over my ass and I exhale.

God, I miss this. I miss this with him.

My hands skate over his back before hooking on his shoulders.

"West," I whisper.

He drags his lips along my jawline. "Yeah, Supernova?" He pulls back and his eyes pin me in place.

Dark and hungry, they cause a shudder to run down my spine.

"I'm sorry," I say, wanting him to know how truly devastated I am that we'll never have more than…this.

His expression softens and he brushes his thumb along my cheekbone. Then, his palm cradles my cheek, and he presses his lips to mine. "Me too, baby." He says it on an exhale, his words washing over my skin like a caress.

Then, his lips are fused with mine and I don't want to come up for air. Instead, I meet him kiss for kiss. He pushes the straps of my dress off my shoulders and peels it down my frame, until it lands in a pool around my feet. I step out of it, losing my heels in the process. I unzip his pants and push them down his hips.

West kicks off his shoes and pants as I make quick work of the buttons on his shirt.

"Jesus, you've been working out," I comment as I push the material off his shoulders.

He chuckles but his eyes are drinking me in like he'll never get his fill. "Missed this tight body," he replies, skimming his palm along the side of my frame until he grips my waist. He squeezes tightly before his hands caress me like he's memorizing the lines and curves of my body.

Gentle fingertips dust along the tops of my breasts. The skate of his palms along my arms and up my ribs. The feel of his mouth moving over the column of my neck as he gathers me to his chest.

When West lifts me, I instantly wrap my legs around his waist. I take his beautiful face in between my hands, gaze into his eyes, and press my mouth to his.

Our kiss is long and soulful. It's filled with the words we won't say, with the promises we know better than to make. West moves us through his condo I still want to check out and toward the bedroom. I don't get a good glimpse of anything since he never stops kissing me. Instead, he holds me closer, I dip my tongue into his mouth, and he moans in a way that sets my body on fire.

West lays me in the center of the bed. His gaze darkens as his eyes scan my frame, lingering on my naked breasts and the delicate, cream-colored lace between my legs. He reaches out, brushing two fingers over my core, up the center of my abdomen, before pinching my nipple.

I gasp and my guy smirks. "You're always so responsive, Nova." He drops to his knees next to my frame. "Drives me fucking mad."

"Only with you," I admit, squeezing my thighs together as my need mounts.

West growls. "Better just be me," he bites out.

I don't correct him. I don't say anything.

His eyes flash and then, he's hovering over me. West presses an open-mouthed kiss to my shoulder before moving down my body. He draws my breasts into his mouth, laving my nipples with his hot tongue as I squirm. His hands grip and squeeze, touch and take.

"West," I whimper, my fingers raking through his curls. Tugging.

"Taking my time, Nov," he murmurs, drawing one of my legs up until my knee bends. He hooks it over his shoulder and gives me a grin. "Missed your taste, baby." Then he dips his head, yanks my lace thong to the side, and drags his tongue up my center.

I suck in a deep breath, the nerves in my body going haywire.

It's been so long. Too damn long.

And no one has ever made me see stars like West Crawford. I've never wanted a man the way I want him.

I've never loved anyone else. With him, it's always been different. More.

He flicks his tongue over my clit and I cry out. Then, he moves lower, using his big hands to spread my thighs, and bury his face against my pussy.

"Shit," I swear, my hips bucking off the bed.

"So damn good," West murmurs, his lips still pressed against me.

"West," I pant, clutching his hair.

He chuckles and touches me gently as his tongue laps at my clit. Then, he pushes two fingers inside, dragging them in and out slowly, while sucking on the little bud.

Just the way I like it. Just the way he does it.

The pressure mounts and I arch my back. My eyes squeeze shut as West brings me to the brink. He smacks his lips, like he's eating his favorite meal. His fingers keep up a relentless, steady rhythm. In and out. His tongue flicks against me expertly as he sucks, savoring my taste.

"Jesus," I cry again, yanking his hair.

And then, I shatter. My body breaks apart as delicious tremors wrack through me.

"That's it, Nova. Break apart for me. God, you're so fucking sexy," West murmurs, pulling back to watch me, even as his fingers continue to tease, wringing out my orgasm as I try to regulate my breathing.

As I come down from the orgasmic bliss, I blink at him. He's watching me, his dark eyes unreadable. West brings his two fingers to his lips and puts him in his mouth, pulling them out slowly as he cleans them off.

I moan and reach for him. He grins and shakes his head. "Not done with you."

"West, I want to—" I reach for him. For his hard length, pointing at me like the needle of a fucking compass. I'm true north. But for how much longer?

My breath lodges in my throat. God, I missed him. He's so big. So fucking hard. So goddamn good. I drag my fingers over his shaft and he sucks in an inhale. I grip him and slowly pump my hand.

West moves closer, kneeling beside me as I roll onto my side and bring his cock to my mouth. I drag the tip along my lips and he swears, his eyes blazing. Then, I lower my mouth down his length and begin to suck. He lets me bob my head a handful of times before he pulls me off, rolls over, and places me on top, straddling him.

"Ride me, baby." It's a command.

I touch him one more time, lining him up at my entrance, before I sink down on his hard length.

"Fuck," he swears, his eyes nearly rolling back in his head.

I gasp, dropping one palm in the center of his chest to brace my body weight. I begin to move, setting a pace I know he'll love. By the way his breathing ticks up, he's enjoying the view.

My hands skate up my body until I touch my breasts, rolling my nipples in between my fingers.

"Nova," West moans.

"Like what you see?"

"Fucking love it," he groans out. And then, he wheezes. "Is this your move? I've seen it before."

I snort before moving faster. West swears.

Before he can flip us again, I pull my body up, standing and spinning, before sinking back on his hard cock.

"Fuck, baby," he swears as I begin to move. I set the same relentless pace, but this time, I give West a perfect view of my ass. I'd hardly call the Reverse Cowgirl my move, but in this moment, I'm claiming it. Working West over, I turn my head to watch as his mouth drops open.

His palm skims over my hips, my ass. He spreads my cheeks and watches as I take his cock.

Then, he groans, "Jesus, baby. Ride me. Take every inch."

So I do. I ride him hard, until we're both swearing and panting.

Then, West flips us again. I have no clue how, but he manages to push me forward. My hands and knees sink into the soft mattress as West grasps my hip. He hikes up his right leg, planting his foot next to my frame, and begins to pound into me. He's so hard and I'm so wet, so fucking needy.

My second orgasm builds and I sink my teeth into the forearm he's got wrapped over my shoulders, to muffle the cries that want to escape.

"West!"

"Come for me, baby." Another demand. "Get there, Nova."

"I am!" I cry out. "I'm coming, West," I tell him as my body unravels a second time.

Two more pumps and then, West swears. "Nova!" My name is a prayer on his lips as he empties inside me.

Then, he collapses next to me and draws me into his arms. His sticky mess coats my inner thighs, but I don't care. Right now, I'm sated. At peace. I turn in his arms and let my eyes close.

"I miss your moves, baby," he says softly.

"I fucking miss you, West."

"Gotta clean you up," he murmurs at some point.

"Hmm," I mumble.

I feel a warm washcloth move over my thighs.

"Nov?"

"Yeah?" I mutter.

"You still on birth control?" West asks. Shit, we didn't use a condom.

Well, wouldn't be the first time. "Yes," I reply.

"'Kay. That was…" He pauses to kiss my shoulder.

"Amazing," I supply.

"Better than amazing."

I open one eye. "Better than a Super Bowl win?"

West chuckles and wraps his arms around me. "This right here? This is the best it ever gets." He kisses the side of my neck. "Sleep, baby."

I do.

I wake with a start. Beside me, West snores slightly. He's naked, his glorious body curled around me. I take a deep breath and shake away the slight headache from too much booze.

Then, I take a moment to study West. The strength of his body, coiled muscles, and strong limbs. The slumber that clings to his expression, his pursed lips, and his long eyelashes.

"I love you, West," I whisper, knowing he's passed out.

Then, I slide from his bed and get dressed in the muted morning light.

My heart feels heavy that I'm walking away.

But what choice do I have? Today, West is heading to a massive amusement park for a parade, my flight leaves in a handful of hours, and we both know it's over.

Hell, it's been over.

My stomach clenches and my body feels heavy.

Then why is it so hard? Why does this feel impossible?

I try to pull myself together in the bathroom but, let's be honest, I look like I'm doing one hell of a walk of shame.

Shit. I slap a hand over the hickey West left over my right breast.

A souvenir. I snort. But even that will fade in time.

Sighing, I check my phone. I ignore the messages from Dad and my brothers. Instead, I text Allegra.

Me: You awake?

Allegra: Obvi. Need a ride?

Me: Can you bring sweats?

Allegra: Duh. Meet you in ten?

Me: Here's the address.

I share my location.

> Allegra: Got it. Breakfast?

My stomach rolls.

> Me: Advisable.

> Allegra: See you. X

I drop my phone into my clutch, grab my heels, and take one last, lingering look at West. I study the navy sheets and the dark wood frame of his bed. He doesn't have any artwork or personal mementos save for one photo on his nightstand.

Moving closer, I lean down to peer at the picture and gasp.

It's me and him. It was taken last August, days before Dad's heart attack. In fact, it's the last photo West and I took together. We were having a BBQ at Derek and Allegra's new house, and West flew into LA for less than twenty-four hours to surprise me. He had training camp and still, he made me feel like his top priority.

In the photo, I'm sitting on West's shoulders, his hands wrapped around my thighs to hold me in place. My hair is a mess, hanging in clumps around my shoulders. But I'm laughing. My mouth is wide open, and my eyes are bright. West is laughing too. We both look so…happy. Light. In love.

Tears prick the corners of my eyes as I drag my fingertips over the photo. Then, I relocate to the living room. I take a second to note that while it's decorated nicely—in creams and tans—it also lacks warmth. There are no personal touches. No throw pillows or cozy blankets. It contains an emptiness that I feel in my bones because the same desolateness is already spreading through my limbs.

Stop. You had your night. Now get your shit together.

I scrawl West a note, take a deep breath, and leave.

By the time Allegra arrives with an oversized Burnt Clovers hoodie and a steaming cup of coffee, my mascara is running.

"Oh, Nova," she says, pulling me into a hug as I cry.

"I still love him," I admit, gripping her matching hoodie. We look like a fucking disaster.

"I know," she says. "Maybe you can—"

"No," I cut her off, not wanting to entertain false hope. "It's over. I'm going back to Paris today and West is…well, he's living his dream."

Allegra stares at me warily before sighing. "Pancakes?"

I sniffle. "A waffle would be better."

She snorts. "Come on. Let's go eat."

My friend ushers me into Derek's rental SUV and takes me to eat. I turn off my phone, not wanting to see West's disappointed messages when he wakes up and realizes I'm gone.

Instead, I force myself to pack my suitcase. To take a hot shower and blow dry my hair.

That afternoon, I hug Allegra, Derek, and Levi goodbye at the Knoxville airport and board a flight to Paris.

There's no more looking back. There's only the future. Sans West Crawford.

WEST

I'M IN THE CENTER OF AN AMUSEMENT PARK—A PLACE THE KID version of me dreamed of—and I feel like there's nothing to smile about.

"Cheer up, bro. After we hang with Cam the Coyote, you're gonna meet a fucking thunderbolt." Gage bumps my shoulder with his, referencing the Tennessee Thunderbolts mascot.

She left me a note. A fucking note. And slipped away like a damn memory.

"And maybe a dragon," Jag tacks on, gesturing toward the popular figures from kid's cartoons milling about the park.

"There's Coyotes pretzels!" Talon exclaims.

"This your first time at an amusement park?" Avery asks.

Talon shrugs.

I heave out a sigh. I need to snap out of this. I need to embrace this moment.

This was my dream.

"Fuck, let's get him some strippers instead," Talon advises.

Gage snorts and Jag shakes his head.

Two days ago, I would've shot Talon a dirty look.

Instead, I glance at him curiously.

"I was kidding," he says, holding up his hands.

I shake my head. "I don't want a stripper but..."

"But?" Talon quirks an eyebrow.

Avery understands my meaning. "You need to go out, blow off some steam, and forget for a little while."

Gage nods in agreement.

"That'd be nice," I admit, even though there's no way I could forget anything about Nova.

But...just for a night? Could I shake off this awful feeling of...what? Rejection? Abandonment? Loneliness? Whatever it is, I don't like it and I sure as fuck don't want to wallow in it.

I learned to suppress these feelings years ago. After Dad's trial. Mom's death. Life in the foster care system.

Nova going back to Paris shouldn't rattle me like this.

And yet, I feel fucking...bereft.

Jag snaps his fingers and points at me. "Tonight. Let's enjoy our parade and tonight, we party!"

Cohen sighs but manages a little smirk. His eyes cut to our team captain.

"I'm in," Avery concludes.

"We're all fucking in," Gage decides.

"Tonight," I agree.

Nova's letter swirls through my mind.

It's too hard to say goodbye again.

Last night was perfect. It's just how I want to remember us.

So proud of you and the man you are, West.

I'll never stop rooting for you, but I want you to move on. Do big things. Have a big love.

Fuck, her words cut me open.

So yeah, I want to forget. At least for a little while.

That night, I'm embracing the moment. And forgetting everything else.

Alcohol buzzes in my veins. The flashes of photographs, the Sharpies pressed into my hand for autographs, the exclamations of congratulations, wrap around me like a protective barrier.

If I can live in this reality, Nova's leaving won't cut so deep.

I cling to it. The fans, the women, the shot glasses brimming with tequila and vodka.

The energy of my team, the vibe in the club.

When Jag invites a slew of women to join us, I don't turn away how I usually do. Instead, I step up and mix drinks.

Vodka sodas. Cranberry vodkas. Vodka shots.

It's all on the menu and I crack jokes as I pass out beverages. When I'm drinking, I'm a hell of a lot friendlier, chattier, and funnier. It's just that, I don't get blitzed often.

Instead of being Nova Martin's boyfriend, I step into the role I shed at some point in the last year.

West Crawford, football player. UCLA campus hero. Coyotes Rookie. Super Bowl winner. Funny, friendly, and free.

The liquor flows like water, the music blares, and as the mood of the crowd spikes, so does my outlook.

Nova gave me closure; I should be grateful.

Nova stepped up for me when no one else did. That is beautiful.

Nova was my college chapter; now, I'm in the League. Literally.

When a busty redhead perches on my knee and demands we take a selfie, I smile.

When a sexy brunette pours tequila between my lips, I open my mouth wider.

As the cameras flash and the comments roll, I become the life of the party.

And I don't look back.

In fact, the next day, I silence my social media notifications and head to LA, where my old football team welcomes me with open arms and raucous applause.

Right now, it's time to party.

Isn't that what she said?

Do big things.

Well, I've got moves too.

"What's good, Vegas?" I shout from the DJ booth.

The club goes wild. Cheers and applause. Women flashing me while their men give me props.

"Damn, you got fans," the DJ says, grabbing the mic.

I laugh. "Yeah."

As I gaze out over the crowd, disbelief rocks my system. People move, their bodies gyrating with the beat the DJ drops. It's a sea of energy, a wave of spontaneity I want to surf.

"Get out there!" Talon grips the back of my neck and gives me a little shove.

Avery's already moving through the crowd, parting it like the Red Sea.

It's mayhem. It's insanity.

It's the perfect environment to lose myself.

Two weeks ago, the Coyotes won the Super Bowl. Since then, I've partied my ass off, in cities across the country, with beautiful women. Little by little, my heartache over Nova's disappearing act has dulled.

With each shot of tequila, I let some of my hurt over our failed relationship go. At every beach party, I come out of my shell a little more, talking with women, laughing with the guys, posing for selfies.

I'm hailed on college campuses—even by my old rivalries

—like a goddamn hero.

Women slide into my DMs like I'm offering a flash sale of designer purses.

My socials are blowing up, my phone pings constantly, and I'm at the center of it all.

My old college buddies were right. There's no time for a girlfriend when I'm playing in the League. There's too much temptation, too many wanting women, a fuck ton of vices.

And right now, I've earned them. I want to take a crack. I'm so damn tired of showing up, leveling up, pushing myself. I did everything right, checked all the boxes, and right now, it's time to enjoy the fruits of my labor.

I step onto the dance floor and open my arms wide.

Talon snickers as women literally fall into them.

Wrapping my arms around a gorgeous blonde and a sinful brunette, I grin. "What're we getting into tonight, ladies?"

The brunette smirks and drags a long red fingernail down my abdomen. "You tell me, West."

Yeah, I'll tell her all right.

"Fuck." I wake up the next morning with a slamming headache and cotton-dry throat.

I groan as I roll to my side and grope for my phone. It scatters across the end table, falling to the floor with a thud.

"Shit," I swear, burying my head in a pillow.

With my eyes squeezed shut, memories from the night before flicker through my mind.

The dark club with the sick beats.

Shots of tequila.

A wet T-shirt contest. Was I the judge?

A topless woman in the jacuzzi tub of my hotel.

Yeah. She won. I picked her.

Damn.

I dangle my arm over the side of my bed, feeling around the floor for my phone. Instead, my fingers catch on a set of keys.

What the hell? I pick up the keys and groan again as the I note the Mercedes Benz keyring.

"Yo!" Talon flings open the door to my room and bounds inside.

I shield my eyes from the light pouring in from the living room of our suite.

"Damn, you're wrecked," he laughs, plopping down on the chair in the corner of my room.

"These your keys?" I lift the keyring higher.

Talon's eyes widen. "You don't remember?"

"Remember what?"

"Dude, you bought a fucking Benz last night. Traded in your shitty truck and finally upgraded."

"What?" I lurch up in bed and the nausea in my gut swims up my throat. "That's impossible." I shake my head, swallowing hard. "I—"

"Auctioned your ride off on some stupid social media event," Talon explains.

I narrow my eyes. Snippets of a conversation—

"You think you can drive my ride?" I laughed.

"Come on! It's for a good cause," the woman holding the phone in my direction explained.

I shrugged. "Whatever, babe. It's yours. I'm upgrading."

But fuck, if it doesn't cut. Tillie can't be replaced. Except, I traded her in for...

"What kind of car did I buy?"

Talon grins. "Benz AMG G 63."

I drop back to my bed and close my eyes. "I'm a fucking douchebag."

Talon chuckles. "Yup. Just enjoy it, man. You got a sick ride. A fucking Super Bowl ring. Women are throwing themselves at you. Trust me, this shit doesn't last. Ride the damn wave and stop bitching. We're heading to Miami tonight."

My phone skitters across the floor with an incoming call.

Talon, good man that he is, gets up to grab my phone and pass it to me. He checks the screen and laughs. "Callie James. Man, you don't want to keep her waiting."

I answer my agent's call. "Hey, Cal."

"Don't butter me up, Crawford. You're off the rails," she admonishes.

I wince. "No hello?"

"You gave away your truck on social media!"

"I just learned that too," I admit.

Callie sighs. "You had an exceptional first season, West."

"Yeah."

"Don't blow it now."

"Hey! I'm just having some fun—"

"Too much fun," Callie cuts me off. "Your image is going to become an issue if we don't get ahead of the curve."

Shit. I sit up again. This doesn't sound good. "What are you talking about?"

"The parties, the women, the drinking—none of this is new for a professional athlete. But it's not your brand, West. You came up as the hardworking, committed, loyal player."

"I still am. I haven't missed anything. Not one commitment."

"Yet." Callie sighs. "I spoke with the head of a PR company this morning. She specializes in crafting the desired reputation for celebrities, professional athletes…"

"What are you getting at?" I cut to the chase.

"How would you feel about going on a few dates with Marisa Mella?"

I frown. "The model?"

Marisa Mella is a gorgeous woman and currently, the face of several powerhouse luxury brands.

"Yes," Callie says, not elaborating further.

"Why?" I ask.

"If the press thinks that you're moving into a relationship, something stable, it could help with endorsement deals. There's money on the table, West. Opportunities for you to grow wealth, to represent labels. But they need to trust that you're not going to embarrass their brand. And, right after winning a Super Bowl, you doing a personality one-eighty, becoming a meme, and a trending hashtag on socials, isn't helping."

I sigh, tapping my head back against the headboard. Endorsement deals are a game changer. And Callie's right, with the season I had and the potential for the future, I am leaving money on the table. It's short-sighted of me to blow opportunities for a handful of weeks fucking around.

"Okay," I say after a long pause.

"Seriously?"

"Yeah," I agree.

"And you're committed? Because this is a business arrangement. There will be a contract. You and Marisa will both be obligated to show up to certain events together, to have a few dinners, that kind of thing."

"I get it. But—" An awful thought occurs to me.

"No. You don't have to do anything…intimate with her," Callie shuts my thoughts down before they have time to grow.

I snort. "'Kay. Thanks, Callie."

"Get your head back in the game, West. You had a few weeks of fun. It's time to rein it in, cultivate the perception of a new, stable, committed relationship with a well-liked and successful woman, and start gearing up for offseason conditioning."

"I get it."

"Good. I'll be in touch with the contract. See you soon, West. And, nice car."

I snort. "Later, Callie."

"Fuck," I mutter to myself as I scroll through my phone.

I'm tagged in thousands of photos from the night before.

And Callie's right—the photos look like I'm some drunk, womanizing, party boy, living up to every negative stereotype assigned to elite athletes.

"You ready for Miami?" Avery asks, appearing in the doorway. He's wearing a pair of swim trunks decorated with sea turtles.

I lift an eyebrow. "That how you're flying?"

Avery chuckles. "I'm hitting the pool this morning. Our flight is tonight."

I shake my head. Callie's words a warning in my mind. "I gotta sit this one out. Head back to Knoxville."

Disappointment flickers through Avery's eyes. "You sure?"

"Yeah, man. But you and Tal have a good time."

Avery shrugs and tips his head. "At least come to the pool party. One last hurrah."

One last hurrah.

The words cause a phantom ache in my chest as they echo in my mind.

I force a smile. "Yeah. I'll catch you up there in a few."

One last party. One last hurrah.

And then, I'll put my head down and get back to work.

HE AUCTIONED OFF HIS TRUCK.

Tears prick the corners of my eyes.

Ugh. Stop being so emotional.

I blink rapidly.

Of course West upgraded his ride. He's a professional football player who is making more money than he's ever had access to in his life. Why shouldn't he indulge and enjoy it?

But seriously? For some random woman to get a nose job?

It wasn't even a good cause…

The next image that pops up on my feed is West with two women perched on his lap. One of them has her fingers threaded through his curls and it's like a sucker punch to my gut.

A tear falls, slowly rolling down my cheek.

"Stop it," I hiss, wiping the tear away.

A reel appears with West's hands moving over a woman's body while on a busy dance floor in some club.

I groan and close my eyes.

Pulling in a deep breath, I remind myself that I'm moving on. I'm in a good place. Over the past few weeks, my brothers have endorsed all my ideas for the tasting room renovation and design. I've been getting the space—a cute little storefront on a cobblestone street near the Champs-Élysée—ready to receive potential customers. My vision is coming to life, and I need to focus on that.

Not West Crawford and his Vegas-bender.

Opening my eyes, my finger hovers over the unfollow button.

"It's time," I murmur. Then, I unfollow West. After that first press, it become easier, and in under five minutes, I've essentially blocked West's social media presence from my feeds. "And now it's done."

"Nova!" Gabe calls out.

I look up from the wallpaper samples in front of me. "Back here."

My brother appears in the curved doorframe. "Wow," he mutters, looking around the space. "It's really coming together."

I place my phone facedown beside the wallpaper book and manage a smile. "Yeah. I can't wait until it's open. I think having a tasting room here will encourage more storeowners and restaurant owners to sample our products on their own time. Sometimes, it's tough to get their attention by showing up at their place of work."

Gabe nods slowly. "Dad's coming around to your way of thinking too."

I snort. "Dad shouldn't be making any business decisions at the moment."

Gabe dips his head. "He's not going to let his health keep him from work much longer."

"I know. But I worry about him. He pushes himself too hard."

"That's not what brought on his heart attack."

I give my brother an incredulous look. "Stress?"

"Poor eating habits, genetics, smoking..." Gabe ticks off other reasons on his fingers.

"We're getting sidetracked," I say, changing the topic. My

brothers accuse me of hovering over my father, but as the only daughter in a house of men, it comes naturally. And I do worry. Dad is my last parent and I don't want to lose him prematurely. Especially if I'm able to help alleviate some of his stress and contribute to our family business. "The point is, I have a lot of good ideas. And you should all listen to me more often."

Gabe chuckles. "I guess so." His eyes scan the storefront again. "I'm proud of you, Nov. You're doing a hell of a job."

"Thank you."

"And I saw on the calendar that you're meeting with Pierre Bernard this week."

"I am!" I grin. Pierre Bernard owns three of the most influential restaurants in Paris. He inherited them from his late father and my family has been trying to sell our wine in the Bernard-owned restaurants for years.

"Dad's going to love that."

"See?" I give a little dance. "You guys need me. I'm the closer."

My brother snorts. "We're all happy you're home, Nova."

His words are reassuring. I cling to them. In fact, I need them after saying goodbye to West. This time last year, I was considering pressing pause on my life to follow West to wherever he was drafted. The thought of not being his was so gut-wrenching that I would have moved to any city and carved out any career path just to be with him.

And now, he auctioned off Tillie for a random woman's cosmetic surgery.

No, I made the right decision by staying in Paris. By helping my family's business. By coming home.

I take a deep breath and my shoulders drop an inch. My eldest brother, Jacques, calls out his arrival.

"Back here!" Gabe and I yell in unison.

Jacques appears with a brown paper bag. He holds it up. "Lunch?"

My stomach growls in response. "Perfect timing."

Gabe reaches into a crate that I swiped from the vineyard for photo-taking purposes and pulls out one of our standard wines. He uncorks it. He looks around the space, still half under construction.

"We can have a picnic-potluck-casual-thing," I say, clearing a spot on one of the long, wooden tables that's piled with sample materials.

Jacques pulls takeout containers from the bag. "I got Croque Monsieur, Croque Madame, and a few salads."

"Perfect." I grab a roll of paper towels.

Gabe pours us each a glass of wine and we stand around the worktable.

Jacques holds his glass in the air, his eyes darting around the new space. "To your new venture, Nova. We wouldn't have considered doing all of this"—he gestures around the space—"without you at the helm."

I smile. My brothers sure know how to build me back up and the truth is, I'm grateful for their support. Right now, I need someone to believe in me and with my family behind me, it makes moving on from West a tiny bit easier. More manageable.

"To the Martins," I reply, mentioning our family and our wine label.

"*Santé.*" Gabe clinks his glass against mine.

We all take a sip of the dry Chardonnay and dig into our lunch.

"So, Pierre Bernard?" Jacques asks.

Gabe and I laugh.

"We're meeting on Friday," I explain.

"He's coming here?" Gabe tilts his head.

I shake my head. "We're having dinner at Le liège."

Gabe's eyebrows lift. "That's fancy."

I shimmy my shoulders. "He's wining and dining me," I joke.

Jacques narrows his eyes. "He's certainly going to flirt with you. Pierre is—"

"A charismatic businessman," I interject, sidelining my brother's protectiveness.

Gabe sighs. "Just, be careful."

"And call if you need us," Jacques adds.

I smirk. "You do realize I'm an adult woman who has dated, correct?"

"Yes," Gabe says slowly. "And, most recently, an adult woman nursing a heartbreak."

I wince at the reminder.

Gabe's expression softens. Jacques reaches out and squeezes my forearm.

I sigh. "Maybe having dinner with Pierre will be good for me. On a personal level. I need to get back out there."

Jacques chuckles. "Can't you find a normal, nice family guy? Why does it have to be a superstar in the NFL or the top restaurateur in Paris?"

I smirk. "I have high standards."

"I'll agree with that," Gabe says, taking a sip of his wine. He looks at Jacques. "Did you give her a budget for this?" His free hand twists in a circle around the room.

Jacques's eyes widen in alarm.

I snicker. "You guys! I got this. Just, trust me, okay?"

Jacques is quiet for a long moment. "We do trust you, Nova. But, a word of warning, business and matters of the heart rarely mix. Be careful with Pierre."

I tip my head in acknowledgment of his concern. "I'll be fine. Now, pass me some salad Niçoise."

My brothers and I enjoy the rest of our lunch talking about business, our dad, and weekend plans. It's easy and familiar, even though I haven't lived in Paris for the past six years.

As I enjoy my wine and laugh with Gabe and Jacques, a feeling of contentment washes over me. I made a choice to come to Paris. Now that I'm here, I'm going to carve a career path out of my family's business, from my father's legacy.

It may not be the career I once dreamed up. I may not be building my future with West at my side. But I'm okay. I'm learning and growing and evolving. I have my family and their support surrounding me.

For the first time in weeks, my phone is silent from West's constant social media notification updates. I allow myself to take a deep breath, let it out, and be present in the moment.

On Friday, I'll meet Pierre Bernard. I'll be charming and persuasive. I'll convince him to sell my family's wine in his restaurants, closing the business deal Dad, Gabe, and Jacques have yet to manage. And in the process, if there's some wining, dining, and harmless flirting, I'll embrace that too.

If West can party in Vegas, why shouldn't I enjoy a delicious meal with a handsome, French businessman?

"Oh, I love this one," I tell Pierre on Friday night, picking up the glass of red he just poured me.

"Are you going to compare it to one of your family's pinot noirs?" he teases.

I grin in reply and take a sip of the bold variety, savoring the hints of cherry that lingers on my tongue. While my brothers and I speak English to each other, and Dad and I speak a mixture of French and English, Pierre and I converse in French. It's been years since I've used French regularly, but the past few months in Paris have helped me regain my fluency. While English is my native tongue, due to my American mom speaking English at home, French is a close second.

Pierre and I are seated in a private alcove at his restaurant and while he arranged our dinner and wine pairings in advance, it's hard for me not to jump in with my sales spiel.

But that would ruin our dinner and make me seem too eager. Too…American for lack of a better word.

Instead, I'm playing it cool. Blasé. Unhurried and unaffected. Tonight, I'm leaning into my French side.

"Hm?" he prompts, winking. Pierre is a good-looking man. With clear blue eyes that crinkle at the corners when he smiles and stylishly coiffed brown hair, he looks younger than his forty-two years. He's fit, with broad shoulders and a trim waist. Well-dressed in a French way that is as casual as it is pulled together. In fact, Pierre is extremely likable.

While he's no West Crawford, and my heart didn't gallop when he kissed my cheeks in greeting, my skin did buzz with an awareness. A spark of something I haven't felt in far too long.

A flicker of relief—mainly that I'm not broken, but also that there's still hope for me—filters through my veins.

"You'll love my family's wines…" I concede, taking another sip. My tongue slips out to catch the drop that clings to my bottom lip. "When you have the pleasure of tasting them." See? I can be fun and flirty. Hell, I was the definition of fun and flirty until West flipped my world upside down and made me love-drunk and foolish.

Pierre's smile widens and he tips his head in my direction. "Touché, Nova." Curiosity colors his irises. "It's an interesting name."

"That's a polite way of inquiring," I laugh. "My mom was an astronomer. Dad was quite traditional in wanting to name my brothers proper, French names."

"Jacques and Gabriel." Pierre nods, well acquainted with my family after years of rubbing shoulders in the industry.

"Exactly."

"But Mom was American and wanted a unique name for her only daughter." I point at my chest. "Since she studied planets and stars, she picked Nova, for Supernova."

Pierre's brow furrows. "Isn't that a dying star?"

I chuckle again. "Technically, yes. But Mom loved the part where it's brighter than any other star in the sky, powerful enough to expel most of its mass, and a fairly rare occurrence in our galaxy." I shrug.

"So she knew you'd be brilliant," Pierre concludes.

My smile slips. "I hope that's what she thought."

His expression softens. "I'm sorry she passed."

"Me too."

"How old were you?"

"Eight," I supply.

He nods. "My mother passed three years ago."

Surprise ripples through me. "I didn't know." I press a palm to my chest. "I'm sorry, Pierre."

"Me too," he repeats my words back to me. Then, sighing heavily, "I'm not sure which is worse. I had her, her love and affection, for many more years than you had your mom. But—"

"You had more to lose," I supply. "Both scenarios suck."

Pierre chuckles, slightly taken aback by my word choice. "Yes," he agrees, raising his wine glass to his lips and taking a long sip. He places down the glass and meets my gaze. "Both scenarios suck. But your mother was right, Nova. You are indeed bright and powerful and unique."

I bite my bottom lip, wondering if he's trying to butter me up the same way I want to impress him—for business purposes. I study his expression, but his eyes are warm and a small smile curls his mouth.

I shake my cynical thoughts away and instead, am flattered by his praise. I dip my head in thanks.

Our entrees arrive a moment later, saving me from having to respond to his thoughtfulness.

Is Pierre flirting with me or are we connecting on a topic we both have experience navigating—the loss of a parent?

Pierre exchanges a few words with the server as awareness sweeps through my limbs, tightening my stomach.

It's been months—hell, more than a year—since a man, other than West, has stirred any physical reaction in me. I bite my bottom lip again and Pierre's gaze darkens.

Uh-oh. I think we are moving into flirting territory.

It's a little scary but a lot exciting.

West sold Tillie. West is living his best life in Vegas.

I can enjoy dinner with Pierre, right? I am enjoying dinner with Pierre.

"I hope you like mussels," Pierre murmurs, pointing at the large bowl filled with mussels in a white wine broth.

"As much as I like fries," I admit, plucking a French fry and popping it into my mouth.

Pierre grins, his smile genuine. "You are a breath of fresh air, Nova. I think we are going to work very well together."

"I hope so," I agree. Satisfaction rolls through my limbs as I realize I'm another step closer to finalizing the deal between my family's wine and Pierre's restaurants.

And what's wrong with mixing a little business and pleasure?

I pick up my wine glass and take a sip.

Absolutely nothing.

"Pierre would like to start selling Martin wine in two of his restaurants," I gloat to Dad and my brothers as I hang up the phone and slip it into the back pocket of my jeans. "I just got the official word."

Dad's eyebrows fly off his forehead, Jacque claps, and Gabe shoves my shoulder affectionately.

"You did it, Nova!" Gabe exclaims.

I breathe on my freshly polished fingernails—shade mint julep—before brushing them against my shoulder playfully.

"Oh, come on. Don't be a big shot about it," Dad says, but he's laughing.

"Years!" I point at the three of them. "You had years. I'm back in town for mere months and—"

"Too late," Jacques cuts me off, glancing at Dad. "Her ego has already exploded."

Dad chuckles and shakes his head. "You're one to talk," Dad tosses back to Jacques.

"Get the paperwork ready." I point at Gabe.

"What am I? Your assistant?" Gabe jokes.

"Should be," I concur.

"Oh, God," Jacques groans.

I laugh and wave goodbye to my family as I move toward

the front door. Today, we had lunch with Dad at our family home, nestled beside the vineyard. "I've got to get back to the city. I have dinner plans tonight."

"With Pierre?" Jacques asks.

"Wouldn't you like to know!" I toss over my shoulder.

"I really would," Dad calls out.

Grinning, I wave goodbye and slip behind the steering wheel of my Peugeot.

I pull away from the circular driveway, casting one last look at my family home. Dad moved us back a few years after Mom's passing and even though I started high school in France, I longed for America. While my brothers spent more of their youth in the United States, they acclimated to France and finished their studies here while I attended two years of boarding school in New England, followed by college in California.

It's been a long time since I've been back but now that I'm here, I realize how much I missed my family. How much I missed having a *home*.

The traffic is heavy on my drive home and by the time I make it into my flat, I'm rushing to shower and dress for dinner. I pull thigh-high chunky boots over my sheer tights and move to slip my phone into my purse when I note a missed call from Allegra, Ivy, and Mckenna. Gah! I forgot about our scheduled group call.

I tap out a quick text.

Me: I suck! I'm so sorry—I totally flaked on the call.

Allegra: Hot date?

Me: Well...

Ivy: STOP! Tell us everything.

Mckenna: Wait, Nova, you're dating? For real?

I snort.

Me: Is that so hard to believe?

Ivy: After West? Kind of!

Me: Don't say his name…

Ivy: Sorry! (grimace emoji face) I forgot he no longer exists.

Me: Better.

Allegra: Refocus. New guy?

Me: It's not a thing. Yet.

Ivy: So, it could be?

Me: Potentially…

Allegra: Who is he?

Me: Pierre Bernard.

Mckenna: (posts photo of Pierre)

Mckenna: This guy?

Mckenna: Wow! He owns a lot of restaurants.

Ivy: Holy shit, Nova. He's hot.

Mckenna: And old.

Ivy: 42 isn't THAT old…

Mckenna: He could be her father.

Ivy: Plus, it's France so…

I snort.

Me: ???

Ivy: Age gaps are hot.

Me: They are!

Mckenna: No comment.

Allegra: Are massively successful men one of your requirements?

Me: Ha! Says the woman dating a ROCKSTAR.

Ivy: Where are you going?

Me: Dinner! Message you after?

Ivy: Duh. We want all the details.

Allegra: All of them.

Mckenna: You can edit as necessary. I don't need to know everything.

I laugh. Kenny is such a prude sometimes.

Me: I'll check in later. Love you, girls.

Allegra: (red heart emoji)

Slipping my phone into my pocket, I grab an umbrella, button up my coat, and step out into the crisp night air to meet Pierre at the restaurant. Tonight, we're having a celebratory dinner—i.e., our first real date.

Giddiness coats my stomach as I near the restaurant. It's not one of Pierre's and it has a wait list months long. The fact that Pierre is taking me to dine here is a big deal and I'm excited to see him and enjoy dinner tonight.

He's waiting for me right inside the door and his blue eyes flash with satisfaction when he sees me.

"Nova." Pierre leans forward, his cologne wrapping around me. It's clean and fresh—a far cry from the woodsy, masculine scent laced with cloves that West wore.

Not thinking about West.

Pierre kisses both of my cheeks. "You look beautiful."

"*Merci*, Pierre." I smile.

A hostess leads us to a table and Pierre presses his fingertips into the small of my back as we walk, me half a step ahead of him.

Once we're seated and the wine is ordered, he beams at me. "You're excited for our new partnership, yes?"

"Very," I agree, my French naturally rolling off my tongue in his presence.

"I'm glad we could celebrate this milestone together."

"So am I." I look around the grand dining room. "Thank you for inviting me tonight. I've heard wonderful things about Roxanne's. I'm thrilled to dine here."

"The pleasure is mine," he assures me.

Our server appears and Pierre rattles off a list of appetizers and entrees. My eyebrows rise but he flicks his hand dismissively, ensuring that we try most of the menu.

Our wine is served.

"To us," Pierre toasts.

"To us," I repeat, clinking my glass with his.

Then, I take a long sip of the delicious wine and—nausea crawls up my throat.

I place my glass down and suck in a breath, hoping to squash the unsettling feeling. But the rich scent of food wafting from the table beside us assaults my nostrils, twisting my stomach painfully.

I jerk forward, my chest pushing the table closer to Pierre.

"Nova?" Alarm is evident in his tone.

I slap my hand over my mouth. "Excuse me." I manage,

standing and beelining for the bathroom. Except, the room tilts. A wave of dizziness crashes over me and I stumble, catching the toe of my boot on…what? Air?

Shit!

A few patrons stare at me in shock, their mouths dropping open, as they watch me hurry past.

Oh no! Tears burn the backs of my eyes as the dizziness spins.

What if I ruin the reputation for the restaurant? What if my illness—sudden and so fucking inconvenient—costs me the partnership with Pierre?

I barely make it to the bathroom before my knees hit the tiles and I heave into the toilet. The contents of my stomach come up in a lurch and I grip the sides of the toilet, trying to keep myself upright.

Spots appear before my eyes and I momentarily wonder if I'm going to pass out. My skin chills and the back of my neck burns. The tiles bite into my knees and I slip to my butt, resting my forehead against the back of my hand as I try to regulate my breathing.

"Are you all right?" Pierre's voice is soft.

"Fuck," I swear, humiliation rocking through me. "Pierre." I close my eyes, unable to face him. "I am so—"

"Shh," he cuts me off, flushing the toilet and helping me to my feet.

He presses a hand towel into my hand, and I drag it across my mouth.

"I feel terrible," I murmur, averting my gaze. The last thing I want to do is breathe vomit breath on Pierre.

"*Ma chérie*," he soothes, wrapping an arm around my waist. I sag against him, all the strength having left my body along with my dignity. "You're okay."

I shake my head as he leads me to the sink. "You're in the women's bathroom."

He snorts. "No one will mind."

I give him a look.

"I'm not leaving you alone," he continues.

"I can't believe I... I don't even know how..." I trail off, unsure how to explain what just occurred.

"Good thing we didn't eat yet. Everyone would think it's food poisoning."

I groan.

Pierre smiles gently. "Don't worry, Nova. While I am sorry you are feeling unwell, you have nothing else to worry about. Come, I'll take you home and hopefully, in the morning, you will be good as new."

"I hope so," I admit.

I rinse out my mouth and allow Pierre to lead me toward a back door.

"But what about—" I gesture toward the dining area.

"It's all taken care of. My driver has your belongings and he's waiting for us in the back so you don't have to face the masses."

I breathe out a sigh of relief. "Thank you, Pierre. Truly."

"It's nothing, *ma belle*." His voice holds a note of worry that lends gravity to the situation. He's not embarrassed or disappointed. He's concerned...about me.

The realization allows me to sink further into his embrace. Pierre presses a kiss to the crown of my head before pulling open the back door to the car and helping me inside.

We pull away from the restaurant and the waves of nausea and dizziness continue.

My head rolls toward the window as I close my eyes and focus on breathing.

Inhale. Exhale.

Inhale. Exhale.

Pierre chatters in a low tone with his driver.

I thank them both profusely when we arrive in front of my flat. As desperate as I am to rush inside and throw myself on the bathroom floor, I let Pierre help me upstairs. He makes sure I'm safely inside before brushing my hair back from my face.

"Do you need anything, *ma belle*?"

I shake my head, softening at his sweet term of endearment. "I'll be okay."

"I know. Rest tonight and I'll check on you tomorrow."

"Thank you, Pierre," I murmur.

He smiles. *"Bonne nuit*, Nova."

"Good night, Pierre."

I close my apartment door and lock it. Then I collapse on the couch and groan.

My phone buzzes in my purse and I pull it out, scanning the group text.

Mckenna: Robyn and Emily are dating!

Ivy: Your roommates?

Mckenna: Yes! I'm so happy for them.

Allegra: That's amazing. I was waiting for this to happen.

Mckenna: I know, right?

Me: Good for them.

Ivy: You're home? It's so…early.

Ivy: Isn't it early? Hang on—I have Paris time on my phone.

Me: It's early.

Mckenna: Bad night?

Me: I think I'm dying.

Allegra: …

Me: Food poisoning?

McKenna: Oh no. Nova, tell me you didn't get sick at the restaurant.

Me: One of the most sought-after dining experiences in Paris.

Ivy: Shit! Are you okay?

Allegra: Was Pierre mad?

Me: Pierre was a gentleman. It came on so suddenly. I had a sip of wine, smelled the food coming by, and bam—went running for the bathroom.

A moment of silence ticks by before an incoming FaceTime lights up my screen. It's a group call with the girls and the fact that they've seen me at my worst—in the immediate aftermath of West's and my break up—and I can't look worse than that, I answer.

"Are you okay?" Kenny sounds concerned.

I groan in response. "Embarrassed more than anything."

"What did you eat?" Ivy wonders.

"Nothing. I mean, I had lunch at Dad's today, but if he or the boys were sick, someone would have texted me by now."

Allegra stares at me curiously, her eyes narrowed.

"What?" I ask.

"Nova," Allegra says, her tone serious.

I lift my eyebrows.

"When was your last period?" Allegra asks.

"Oh, shit," Ivy mutters.

"No way." Mckenna shakes her head.

"Are you kidding me?" I laugh. "I'm not pregnant, A. I had—" I cut myself off as my mind whirls. When was my last period? I frown.

"Fuck." Ivy tosses a hand in the air.

"Breathe," Allegra demands as another wave of dizziness threatens to drown me. "You're okay."

Didn't Pierre tell me the same thing at the restaurant?

How is everyone in my life so colossally wrong? Clearly, I am *not* okay.

I open the calendar app on my phone and scroll back, waiting for a date and a memory, an event—some combination of both—to give me the confirmation I seek. But… "I'm late," I breathe out, staring at the date of my last period. In fucking January.

"How late?" Mckenna asks.

"Like eight or nine weeks," I admit, trying to do the math and failing.

"Seriously?" Ivy shrieks.

"You didn't notice?" Mckenna wonders.

"Apparently not," I snap, feeling the panic unfurl in my veins.

"You need to take a test," Allegra decides, getting the conversation back on track.

"Oh yeah, let me just grab one from the bathroom," I say sarcastically.

"You usually have spare tests in your makeup bag," Ivy reminds me.

Shit. "You're right." I close my eyes. I've been in this predicament before. My period has never been super regular which is why I keep track of the dates. But, in the past, I took a test more for peace of mind than for abject terror.

Right now, I'm scared as fuck because I know…*I know*… there's a real possibility.

That night, me and West, everything was so familiar. So, *right*. I try to recall moments from that night but all I see is his gorgeous face, the love lining his eyes, and—argh! I can't go there. It hurts too damn much.

We didn't use a condom because I'm on birth control.

But...fuck. With the flight and time change, I skipped a pill. And then I doubled up the following day. Was it too late?

"Go check your makeup bag," Allegra instructs.

I let out a deep breath and clutch my phone as I relocate to the bathroom.

I reach into the cabinet underneath the sink and pull out some of my cosmetic bags. Sure enough, nestled at the bottom of one, is a brand-new pregnancy test.

"See? You're going to be such a prepared parent," Ivy comments.

"Too soon," Allegra says.

I sigh. "Stay on the phone?"

"Duh," Ivy says as Mckenna nods solemnly.

I place the phone on the vanity as I pee on the stick. Then, I lay it flat on the back of the toilet and pull myself together. After I wash my hands, I pick up the phone. "How much time has passed?"

"One more minute," Allegra says.

I stare at my friends' faces and try to remain calm.

My fingers tremble and coldness sweeps my limbs.

Nerves knot in the pit of my stomach and my ears ring.

I am so not fucking okay.

"No matter what happens, you have support," Mckenna reminds me.

"It's going to be negative," Ivy suggests.

"We got you, no matter what," Allegra promises.

"Fuck," I mutter, wiping my hand over my face.

Nerves continue to cluster, causing my shoulder blades to tense, and my neck to pinch. My hands are legit shaking now and my mouth is too dry to produce saliva.

Don't think. Just wait, I mentally chastise myself.

"You can look now," Allegra says.

I pull in a deep breath and warily lean forward to peek at the stick.

A blue plus sign greets me and I freeze.

"Well?" Ivy asks.

"What does it say?" Mckenna demands.

"I'm fucking pregnant," I admit, my voice monotone with shock.

I pick up the stick and squint at it. Angling it to the light, I wonder if my eyes are playing tricks on me. Nope, it's a positive plus sign.

"I'm having a baby," I whisper.

"Congratulations!" Mckenna exclaims.

Ivy clucks, "Too soon."

"Nova?" Allegra's voice sounds faraway. "You're okay."

No, I'm really not.

WEST

"AND THEN, WE'LL HAVE DINNER AT NOBU," MARISA MELLA continues rattling off her demands.

"Whatever," I sigh, kicking back in the conference room chair.

Beside me, Callie straightens. She smiles at Marisa's manager, Claudette, but the corners of her mouth are pinched. "West loves Nobu."

I snort but at Callie's arched eyebrow and stern expression, I nod in agreement.

"Also, Marisa has a fashion show for Hansen Cross in late spring that we'd like West to attend. I don't have the exact dates, but once it's confirmed, I'll let you know," Claudette adds.

I flick a dismissive hand.

"It's in Milan," Marisa says, smiling dreamily. "We could see an opera at La Scala and…"

"Fuck me," I mutter.

Callie glares at me.

The Opera, I mouth.

She sighs. "How about dinner at Ristorante Galleria? There will be a lot of foot traffic and it's a great location to be photographed. Plus, the food is amazing."

"Or I can just watch the fashion show, which will be torture enough. And we can leave it at that?" I tack on.

Marisa gives me a small, understanding smile. "We can figure things out closer to the date."

I let out a sigh of thanks and tune out the rest of the conversation.

Milan. My heart rate quickens.

I'm going to Europe for the first time for a fucking fashion show. And not for a label designed by Nova. But for my fake girlfriend's career.

I'm going to Europe—not to visit Nova or meet her family in France, but to be photographed laughing with Marisa Mella.

I'll be in Europe with a woman who isn't Nova.

The thought tightens my stomach and I shift to wash the discomfort away.

"Anything else?" I interrupt after a few minutes, wanting to get this over with. Over the past week, Marisa and I had a trial of sorts. I flew up to New York City to take her to dinner at a pretentious French restaurant and she came to Knoxville during the week, where we hung out at a coffee shop, before I hit the Coyotes facilities to begin conditioning.

If I'm being honest, hanging with her isn't terrible. She's entertaining and thoughtful. She reads psychological thrillers and loves to travel. She has a younger brother she adores.

It's been…fine.

But there's no spark, no chemistry, nothing to write home about. I mean, if I had a home to write to.

I guess that's the point. We're spending time together for our careers, nothing more, nothing less.

"That's it," Marisa says, standing from the table. She leans forward to shake Callie's hand. "Nice to see you again, Callie." She smiles at me. "Speak soon, West."

"Yep." I nod, stuffing my hands into my pockets and leaning back on my heels.

Callie rolls her eyes. "Very friendly."

I sigh. "It's weird."

"She's a nice woman."

"I guess," I acquiesce.

Callie grins. "How are things going with your teammates? Are you spending more time with the guys?"

"Yeah," I say, dragging a hand along my chin. "I didn't expect so many of my teammates to stay in Knoxville for the offseason."

"A few of them are from here," she explains.

"True. It's been good though. I've been hitting the weight room with Avery and Cohen. I'm going to grab a burger with Gage when he gets into town this weekend."

"Gage is coming into town?" Surprise lights up Callie's eyes.

"Yeah." I shrug, noting the way she purses her lips. "Why?"

She shakes her head slightly. "No reason. I just thought he'd be in Miami longer. Anyway…" She changes the subject. "I'm glad this thing between you and Marisa is working out. I've received a few feelers from two major athletic clothing brands as well as an energy drink company. Keep it up and we'll have a few endorsement deals ironed out before training camp."

I grin. "Hope so."

Callie pats my shoulder as she walks past me. "See you soon, Crawford."

"'Bye, Cal," I say as she leaves the conference room.

Then, I pull out my phone and text a group chat with some of my teammates.

Me: Anyone hungry?

Cohen: I could eat.

Avery: Where you at?

Me: Downtown.

Cohen: Tacos!

Avery: Done. Meet you guys at Alberto's in twenty.

Me: See you.

Smirking, I slip my phone into my pocket and stroll out of the office building. The bright sunshine and mild climate wraps around me and I exhale.

I'm doing what I'm supposed to do. Connecting with my teammates, making friends, moving on. And it feels good. Even if it will never be right.

The following week passes quickly as I commit to more training sessions with my teammates, escort Marisa to a charity gala in Washington DC, and even make plans to meet up with a few of The Burnt Clovers members for dinner since the band is performing a show nearby.

"Where are you cutting out to early?" Talon asks as I rack the bar.

I blow out a sigh and wipe a towel across my forehead to sop up some sweat. The handful of weeks I had fun, drank my face off, and partied with random women have caught up with me. It's good I'm hitting the gym again and realigning my focus with football. "Meeting some friends for dinner."

"What friends?" Avery smirks.

I flip him the finger.

"Come on, Crawford." Cohen places a hand over his heart, as if I've wounded him. "Aren't we your besties?"

I shake my head. "I have other friends, you know?"

My three teammates raise their eyebrows and hit me with incredulous looks, not voicing their obvious opposition to that statement.

"A few of the guys in The Burnt Clovers," I explain.

"The rock band?" Cohen asks, curious.

Avery snaps his fingers and points at me. "They came to our game."

Talon nods. "The woman you brought to party with us was in their posse."

"Nova's not in anyone's posse," I scoff.

Cohen angles his head toward mine.

"My ex, Nova, is best friends with Derek's girl, Allegra," I explain. "We became boys and still keep in touch even after…"

"Right," Talon agrees.

The guys continue to look at me and I swear under my breath.

"Would you like to come to dinner?" I extend the invitation.

Cohen's grin widens. "I knew we were your best friends, man."

"I mean, I don't want to put you in an awkward position but…" Avery trails off.

I snort. "We need to leave in twenty."

"I'm calling first shower!" Talon announces, beelining for the locker room.

While there are several shower stalls, the first one on the right has the best water pressure and everyone knows it.

Avery swears and Cohen wipes down the machine he was using with an antiseptic wipe.

We head to the locker room, take quick showers, and dress for dinner.

"I'll ride with you," Avery says as we hit the parking lot.

I give him a surprised look.

Cohen shrugs. "Your new ride is a serious upgrade."

I chuckle but something twists in my chest. I fucking miss Tillie.

Avery slides into the passenger seat of my car and Talon indicates that he'll follow me to Strickland's steakhouse.

I shoot Reign a quick message that I'm bringing a few teammates.

Reign: All good.

Me: Sure?

Reign: Yep. Levi had other plans and Jameson bailed because he's a pussy-whipped bitch.

I pocket my phone and pull out of the parking lot. While the band's animosity toward bass player, Jameson Tate's girlfriend Amelia is well-known, I can't help but feel bad for the guy.

He's so twisted up over her, he can't see straight. And while my college buddies used to rib me about being the same over Nova, I didn't give a shit. Nothing mattered but her. It's a hard predicament to be in—stuck between your found family and the prospect of a real one.

"It's cool we're tagging along?" Avery asks after a beat. His tone holds a hint of uncertainty that's out of character for the celebrated QB.

"Yeah, man," I laugh. "It's cool." I cock my head at him. "What? Are you a fan?"

He shrugs, a slight blush working over his cheeks, and I crack up.

"Shut the fuck up," I mutter, shaking my head.

"They're a solid band," he says defensively.

"Very talented," I agree. "I just never took you for the type to—"

"What?"

I shrug, leaning back in my seat. "I don't know. Get starstruck."

"Appreciating quality music is hardly acting like a groupie."

I groan. "You're not going to ask for an autograph, are you?"

He flips me the middle finger and I chuckle. A genuine laugh. It feels good because I haven't laughed in too damn long.

I valet in front of Strickland's and we walk inside.

Derek "Reign" Reiner and Maverick Tate are already seated and stand as we approach the table. Talon and Cohen are a few steps behind me.

"What's good, man?" Derek slaps my hand and pulls me in for a hug.

"Not much. Just grinding," I admit.

"And partying," Mav laughs, giving me a backslap.

I lift an eyebrow. "You look tan."

"He just got off a flight from Costa Rica," Derek explains.

"*Pura vida*," Mav sighs, dreamily.

I grin and introduce my teammates. To his credit, Avery plays it cool. We take our seats and order a round of drinks.

"Congrats on the big game! That catch was incredible." Mav looks at Cohen.

"Thanks, man. Appreciate that. Where are y'all playing?" he inquires.

Mav dips his head and chuckles. He leans forward and lowers his voice. "It's a private concert."

I lift an eyebrow. "Seriously?"

"I know, right?" Mav nods.

"What kind? A wedding?" Talon guesses.

"A bat mitzvah," Derek says drily.

Cohen snorts.

I shake my head. "You guys are going to have a bunch of tweens passing out trying to take a selfie with you."

Mav laughs as Derek scowls. "Tell me about it," he grumbles.

We fall into an easy conversation about sports, music, and life in general.

We're halfway through dinner when Maverick shares that he's been dating a model.

"Is it serious?" I ask.

Reign gives me a look. "Are any of Mav's relationships serious?"

Mav flips him the bird and looks at me. "We're...having fun. But she did tell me something interesting."

I lift an eyebrow, waiting. But understanding forms in my mind and agitation gathers in my fingertips. I know what's coming—

"Seems you're dating one of her friends. Marisa Mella?" Mav asks.

Derek's eyes narrow on me and his jaw hardens.

What the hell is that about? I know he looks out for Nova since she's one of Allegra's best friends but...I'm allowed to date since we're broken up and all. Besides, Marisa and I have been photographed together. Our images are posted on our socials. It's not like it's a secret.

Avery snorts and takes a swig of his beer. "Yeah, Crawford. Tell us about Marisa?" He lifts a mocking eyebrow.

I sigh and drag a hand over my face. "It's...nothing."

"Not what I heard," Mav mutters.

"It's a PR stunt," I admit, leaning closer and lowering my voice. Here I am, breaking the terms of my contract, because I don't want...what? Nova to think I've moved on? "We're... helping each other out."

"Ah," Mav says knowingly, like he's been in this predicament before.

Reign's expression relaxes slightly. "So, it's fake?"

"Pretty much," I admit.

"Allegra was worried you moved on," Mav shares, confirming my concern.

"And Nova? What does she think?" I ask, hating myself the second the question is out of my mouth.

Reign swears before snapping his mouth shut, as if he's preparing himself for whatever is about to unfold.

I straighten in my seat, restless energy sweeping my limbs. What the hell does Nova think? Is she upset? Or worse—indifferent? Hell, is she dating?

My hands fist as I try to swallow the possibility that she's with another man. Who isn't me. And fuck, it scrapes me raw from the inside out.

"She doesn't know," Reign admits quietly.

"Seriously?" I ask. How the hell does she not know? Callie made sure several photos were posted to my social media accounts.

"She unfollowed you." Mav points at me, answering my unasked question.

"Fuck." Talon grimaces. "That's gotta burn."

I glare at him.

He stuffs a dinner roll in his mouth.

Cohen watches me curiously, a streak of sympathy in his gaze. It makes me feel like a chump, his pitying me.

I curse softly and take another pull of my gin and tonic. "She's free to do whatever she wants; same as me."

"Right," Derek agrees, nodding.

"Is she though?" Mav asks, his tone cryptic.

Derek shoots him a warning look.

"What's going on?" I ask, narrowing my eyes on the band members.

"We gotta tell him," Mav declares, causing my teammates to straighten in their chairs.

A bubble of tension hangs over our table, threatening to burst with each passing second.

"Tell me what?" I snap. "Is she—Is she with someone?"

Horror washes over me as I consider the possibilities of what could be so awful, Derek doesn't want to clue me in.

"Is she engaged? Married?" I ask, my mind whirring. "Fuck—is she pregnant?"

Derek's fork falls from his hand, clattering against his plate before slipping to the crisp tablecloth. Gravy, along with mashed potatoes, stain the white cloth and I narrow in on the expanding circle as nausea rolls in my gut.

Holy shit. Nova's moved on. She's...having a baby? With another fucking man.

The back of my throat burns and pain like I've never known twists my stomach. The space behind my face stings and I feel like I got punched in the throat. I try to clear it but can't manage the sound.

I can't manage anything as I try to process this painful fucking news. I want to jump out of my body. Right now, my skin feels too tight. My lungs incapacitated. I'm...disoriented.

Shit. Focus on breathing. On not passing out and face-planting into my fucking ribeye.

"She is," Derek admits after an agonizing pause.

"Fuck," Avery mutters.

"Damn," Cohen agrees.

"Shit," Talon rounds it out.

I push away from the table. The scrape of the chair's legs along the floor makes an ugly sound and Mav winces, his gaze swinging around to other patrons.

Anyone staring at us respectfully drops their curious eyes.

Derek reaches out and wraps a hand around my wrist, stopping me. "It's yours." His voice is low but firm.

I shake my head because I don't want to hear—

"What?" I gasp. I must have heard him wrong because it just sounded like he said—

"It's your baby, West. She just found out and..." Derek trails off.

Spots appear before my eyes. Relief mixed with terror

and…anger gathers in my stomach like a brewing storm before rolling through my limbs, sweeping through me like a tornado. All consuming. Dangerous. Devastating.

I can't be a father. A hazy memory—one of my father in an orange jumpsuit staring at me through a thick glass partition—flickers in my mind. I used to press my fingertips to his, my hand so much smaller. Because the last time I visited him in lockup, I was seven.

I shake my head to clear it, but it remains, my mother's sharp swearing an echo in my eardrums.

And then, the night she died and—

"Are you sure?" The sharpness in Avery's tone cuts through my memory. His eyes are hard as he glares at Reign. So much for being a fan. Right now, my captain has my back and it allows me to breathe a fraction easier. "Because this isn't something to—"

Derek lifts a hand, cutting him off. His expression holds more understanding and compassion than I'd ever give him credit for. "I know. And I'm sure."

"Jesus," Cohen murmurs.

"What do I—when? I need to see her," I blurt out.

Like your dad gave a shit about your mom?

I ignore that. Because I'm not my dad. I'm nothing like him.

All the guys at the table exchange a long look.

"What?" I demand. I swear if one of them drops one more bomb on my head, I'm going to detonate along with the news.

"Why don't you take a few days and…process?" Mav suggests.

"Fuck that," I reject the rational advice. That's the type of shit my father pulled. Stayed away. Always busy. Fucking selfish. That's not me. "I need to see Nova. As soon as possible."

Talon taps on the screen of his phone.

I glare at him and he looks up.

"There's a flight to Paris tonight. Eleven forty p.m.," he offers.

I nod. "Book me on it."

"I'll drive you home to pack," Avery says, holding his hand out for my keys.

"You just want to drive his ride," Cohen taunts.

Mav grins. "It's a sick ride."

"Thanks," I mutter, my eyes cutting to Mav and then, Derek. "Thank you. For telling me."

They both nod. Derek's expression is graver than Mav's.

"Maybe you should give her a heads-up?" Derek suggests.

"No." I shut it down. "Please, don't tell her I'm coming. I need, I need to do this my way. I deserve the chance to hear it all—well, everything else—from Nova. Without anyone else weighing in or offering advice."

Derek holds my gaze for a long moment, his eyes studying mine. "Fair enough," he finally agrees.

Mav pretends to drag a zipper along his lips and tosses the keys.

Reign snorts. "Yeah, like you're a fucking secret keeper? You spilled the beans." He points at me.

Mav shrugs. "He has a right to know."

"Yeah," Derek agrees softly. He looks at me again. "You deserve to know."

"Let's go. We need to hurry if you're going to pack and make it to the airport on time," Avery says.

I look at Talon and Cohen. "For right now, this stays between us." I gesture around the table.

"Circle of trust," Cohen swears.

"We got your back," Talon declares.

His words ease some of the knots in my stomach. I'm so used to being on my own that right now, having my team-mates, hell having Derek and Mav fill me in, is a relief.

But it's short-lived as the truth sinks in and rattles me to my core.

I'm going to be a father. A dad!

Fuck, I pray I'm nothing like my poor excuse for a sperm donor. Still serving life for a murder too gruesome to dissect. He's fucked-up, twisted, and not worthy of my thoughts.

I mutter my thanks and follow Avery out of the restaurant. I let him drive me home in my own car as my thoughts spin.

Nova's pregnant with my baby.

And she didn't fucking tell me.

WEST

THE FLIGHT TO PARIS IS THE LONGEST TEN HOURS OF MY LIFE. My head spins, my hands stretch and fist, as if looking for purchase on something tangible, and a lump of—so much damn emotion—fills my throat.

Nova is pregnant. We're having a baby. She didn't tell me.
Is she scared? Sick? Worried about the future?
Is she happy? Excited? Dreaming up baby names?

The fact that I don't know any of it—probably wouldn't have a goddamn clue if not for Reign and Mav—heightens my anger and intensifies my concern.

I need to see her. I need to *know*.

Reign: Driver's waiting for you. Check your email for a hotel reservation. Take it if you need it. Leave it if you don't.

Reign: A and I are hoping you leave it.

Me: Did Allegra give Nova a heads-up?

Reign: Not yet. This is up to you, man. Do your thing.

Me: Thanks.

Me: For everything.

Reign: No sweat.

The second I land, I slip into the hired car Derek arranged. He also sent me an email with the details for a hotel confirmation at The George-Louis Hotel in Paris. I slip my phone into my pocket and look up.

The driver makes eye contact with me in the rearview mirror before looking away. There's no way he recognizes me. No one over here gives a shit about football.

American football anyway.

"Vineyard Martin, yes?" he confirms.

"Yep," I reply, nodding.

"You know the family?" His voice is heavily accented, but his English is a million times better than my French and I'm relieved I understand him perfectly.

"I do," I say slowly. Then, hope this guy can shed some insight onto Nova's life here. While she told me all about her dad and brothers when we dated at UCLA, I know next to nothing about her life since she moved to France. "Not very well though. Are you from this area?" I gesture out the window.

"Oh, no," he chuckles, shaking his head. "But everyone knows the Martin family. Claude Martin's vineyard has been in his family for generations. Then, he moved to America and his uncle started to take care of the property." The driver's nose wrinkles. "Wine started going downhill. And then, Claude was back." He grins. "He is an excellent vintner."

I frown. What the fuck is a vintner? Or is that French for…

"Winemaker," the driver explains and I nod appreciatively.

"And his kids?" I dig.

The driver's smile widens. He looks like he'd be a good father. Laugh lines bracket his mouth, his eyes crinkle at the corners, and there isn't an ounce of stress rolling off his shoulders. He's…pleasant. "His sons are also talented. Jacques takes after his father more. Gabriel has done well to expand the brand and make it more well-known in other parts of the country, and international."

We're quiet for a moment.

I clear my throat. "And his daughter?"

The driver's eyes light up with amusement as they flicker to mine again. He holds my gaze for a long moment before gazing back at the road.

"Ah, I see. The daughter, Nova, yes?"

"Yeah."

"She is…"

I hold my breath as he trails off. Is he going to say successful? Beautiful? *Pregnant*?

All three would be true and right now, I want to know anything I can glean about Nova. I want to know how people here—in her hometown—view her. What do they think about my supernova?

"A breath of fresh air," the driver admits. "She came home and reinvigorated the vineyard. She takes good care of her father and of course, her brothers. But her business sense…it's very good," he admits. "She is strong and nurturing." His eyes meet mine again. "She's a wonderful woman."

Ah, fuck. Does he have a crush on her? He looks old enough to be her dad but… Nova once joked that age gaps are hot. I narrow my eyes. "You know her and the family well?"

He chuckles. "I do. I have worked for them for over twenty years."

I rear back, surprised. "You work for the Martins?"

"Yes, I am Michele, Claude's personal driver."

What the hell? My stomach tightens and my chest squeezes painfully.

I clear my throat, as I pull out my phone. "It's nice to meet you," I grit out.

> Me: I thought you didn't tell Nova I was coming.

> Reign: Hi, West! It's Allegra.

I groan. Allegra blew up my spot, didn't she?

> Reign: Paris is beautiful this time of year, isn't it?

I glare at the phone screen.

> Reign: Anyway, Nova doesn't know you're in town. I told her dad you wanted to surprise her. You should meet him, West. He's a good man and you'll need him on your side.

> Me: You're interfering.

> Reign: I know.

> Me: You think I'll need him because…

> Reign: Because Nova's overwhelmed. And her dad, he understands her in a way no one else does. He'll know how to handle things.

> Me: He doesn't know? About the—

I backtrack, deleting my message. Why can't I write it?
The baby.
Gah! I can barely think it.

> Me: He doesn't know everything?

Reign: No.

Me: Why are you helping me?

Reign: I know you love her, West. And you deserve to know that you're having a baby. Just, go easy on Nova. This has been hard for her.

How hard? I want to ask. But I don't.
Instead, I tap out a reply.

Me: Got it. Thanks for arranging the ride and hotel.

Reign: Anytime. Good luck, West.

Reign: I'm rooting for you.

Reign: That looks fucking weird. Allegra's rooting for you, man. And I hope you don't crash and burn too.

I scoff and slip my phone back into my pocket.

"Here we are," the driver announces, pulling down a long, windy road.

The vineyard stretches around us, rows upon rows of grapevines spread as far as I can see. And then, the space before us opens up and the most beautiful home I've ever laid eyes on appears.

A sweeping stone structure that looks like a castle and a manor birthed a baby. Arched windows, a tiled roof, and a massive door. Flower boxes bloom with color beneath each window. It's...beautiful. It's like I stepped back in time and entered a new reality.

Nova Martin's family owns a goddamn vineyard.

"Whoa," I exhale.

Of course, I knew that Nova's family had a vineyard, but she made it seem like it was a small, tucked-away winery. That it's as much of her family's business as it is their passion project. I sure as hell wasn't expecting...this.

Michele slows into the circular driveway and parks. He moves from the car and I scramble to exit and grab my suitcase before he can do anything else for me. I feel like I'm being waited on hand and foot and while I'm certainly not used to it, I don't like it either.

"West Crawford," a man calls out, his English heavily accented with French.

I look up into the face of Claude Martin and freeze. He's a towering presence, tall and lean and formidable. He grasps the doorframe and I recall his recent health issues.

A heart attack that flipped Nova's world upside down. By extension, mine too.

"Mr. Martin." I step forward, extending my hand. "I'm sorry to show up unannounced and—"

"Nonsense!" He swats my hand away and pulls me into a hug. "I knew you were coming."

The breath whooshes out of my lungs as he gives me a squeeze. I clap him on the back.

Fuck. Is this what dad hugs feel like? Because for a second, it's as if he held me together. Glued all the broken fragments rattling around inside of me into a whole. Reminded me that I can do this.

I can be a dad.

"Call me Claude." Claude lets go and I feel unsteady on my feet.

I turn to thank Michele, but he's already pulled away, the red taillights getting swallowed up by the rows of vines.

I grip the handle of my suitcase instead, needing something to *do*.

"Come on in. Have a glass of wine," Claude chuckles.

"Nova's going to be so happy to see you." He turns into the house, and I follow him, my eyes widening at the space.

The decor, the artwork, the furniture, everything looks like it was curated specifically for this home. It's cohesive and stunning as much as it's functional and inviting.

Holy shit. It's like I'm in a magazine spread.

There's a throw over the back of an armchair that's clearly been used and yet, it looks perfectly styled where it was tossed.

I shake my head. This is some rich people shit that I've never encountered before.

"I hope so," I admit.

Claude mock winces. "Surprises can go either way with her. But I have a feeling she'll like this one."

I manage a grin even though I feel like vomiting.

"*Salut*." Claude passes me a wine glass and holds his up to clink.

"Cheers," I reply, clinking his glass and taking a sip.

"Have a seat." He gestures toward the kitchen island and my eyes bug out as I take in the spread.

A fancy charcuterie board. A plate filled with…raspberry tarts? Sliced bread—the good, crusty kind I have to buy at a specialty bakery back home.

"This is too much," I mutter.

Claude chuckles. "It's nothing." He leans in closer. "And I can't take credit for it. Our housekeeper, Debbie, arranged everything. I'm happy to meet you, West. I want to get to know the man my daughter's in love with."

My head snaps up at that.

Claude's voice is light, but his eyes are serious.

I work a swallow. "We broke up," I remind him.

He nods slowly, his eyes steady on mine. "And yet, here you are. So, why are you surprising her now, West Crawford?"

Oh, shit. I sit on a barstool and drag a hand over my hair.

I've never had to do this before. The handful of times I've met a girl's parents, I didn't give a shit if they liked me or not. I had nothing to prove. And hell, no women ever met my parents because… I don't have any. Not really.

But this, right now, I hold Claude's gaze. This matters.

"I miss her," I say truthfully. "And Nova and I have unfinished business that I'm not ready to give up on."

"Not yet?" he digs.

I shake my head once. "Not ever."

He continues to stare at me, and I force myself to remain still. At ease. Even though my skin crawls with nerves and my throat pinches painfully.

He's going to find me lacking. How can he not?

His daughter is a…fucking heiress. She's smart and funny. She has a wicked sense of humor and a lightness that lifts the spirits of everyone in any room she enters. She's a brand of life I didn't know existed until I encountered her. And now, I don't want to give it up. Not when I've experienced how good things can be.

I blink.

Claude takes a long sip of his wine and grins. Smacking my shoulder, he takes the barstool catty-corner to mine. "Good answer. I'm glad you're here. How was your flight?" He passes me a slice of bread.

We sit around and talk. Eat. Laugh.

Visiting with Claude, I learn more about Nova's childhood. About how the loss of her mother scarred her well into adulthood. About her desire to attend boarding school to maintain her American roots and her connection to her mom.

I learn that Claude loves her so much, he was willing to let her go across the Atlantic so she can search for whatever she felt was missing. He thinks she found it at UCLA, through her friendships with Allegra, Ivy, and Mckenna.

Through her relationship with me.

That lands like a throat punch. "You think so?" I question.

He nods, polishing off his third glass of wine. "Absolutely. When she met you, something changed. She became more serious and forward thinking; she matured. For the first time, she had something she wasn't willing to compromise on." He smiles at me. "You're good for her, West. I'm happy you're here."

"Thank you," I say sincerely. I glance over my shoulder at the front door. "Is Nova—will she be home soon?"

Claude laughs heartily and checks his watch. "I hope so," he says. "But she won't be coming here. She has a flat in Paris." He gives me an apologetic shrug. "When Allegra called, I was too eager to meet you to have our conversation wait."

Realization dawns and I nod. "I understand. You wanted to make sure I'm here for the right reasons."

"I did," Claude says.

"And I am," I confirm.

"I know that now." He gestures toward the front door and I stand. "Michele will drive you back to Paris. I believe Nova has a business dinner tonight at a bistro. Michele can drop you there and you can meet up with her."

"Thank you, Claude." I extend my hand.

This time, he takes it and gives a firm shake. "Welcome to Paris, West."

Claude walks me out to the waiting car and I stow my suitcase in the trunk again.

"Did you like the wine?" Michele asks as we set off for Paris.

I stifle a laugh. I can't believe I lost half the day I could have had with Nova driving around France to meet her dad. But it was worth it. "Very much."

"Good," Michele says, as if he knows I'm talking about more than the wine.

I turn to look out the window, enjoying the passing

scenery. During the drive, I mull over the tidbits Claude shared about Nova and her life.

God, she's going to be the most incredible mother. Her energy is the kind that believes in magic and fairy dust. She wishes on stars and crosses her fingers behind her back when she fibs.

Nova still maintains a childish streak that allows her to be playful and present in a way that I'm not.

Nah, Dad beat that out of me at a young age and Mom's neglect prior to her death finished the job.

"We're here," Michele announces as we pull up in front of a bistro.

"Thank you, Michele."

"I'll drop your luggage at—"

"Nova's flat," I say before he can suggest the hotel.

His eyes meet mine in the rearview mirror again. I don't blink.

Finally, he nods.

"Thanks again," I mutter, sliding out of the back seat and closing the door.

Then, I turn toward the bistro. A flash of blonde hair through the large, front window catches my attention and I falter.

Then, I fucking freeze.

Because Nova is sitting in the restaurant with a suave man beside her. She looks stunning in a red sweater and big, gold earrings. And he? He's got his fucking arm wrapped around the back of her chair as he turns into her and brushes his thumb along the corner of her mouth.

What the fuck?

She dips her head, her lips parting on a laugh.

And I see fucking red.

"Get your fucking hands off her," a low voice growls, a second before slapping Pierre's arm off the back of my chair.

I suck in an inhale, whirling in my seat to lock eyes with West. His eyes are wild, his nostrils flared, and his expression bathed in…pain.

"West?" I mutter, standing from my chair. Surprise rolls through me as my heart hammers. What is he doing here?

My eyes widen as the anger rolling off him in waves wraps around me.

Oh, shit. *Does he know? How?*

Behind me, Pierre stands as well. His hand settles on my hip as he tries to maneuver me behind him in the cramped space, crowded with other patrons. I feel their eyes swing and narrow in our direction.

"Is that Pierre Bernard?"

"Ooh, with Claude Martin's daughter?"

"I've seen him before. Does he play a sport?"

"Is she back in Paris? I thought she lived in America."

Jesus. We're making a spectacle. The last thing I need is for parts of my personal life to become public knowledge.

Pierre's hand is yanked off my hip. "I said, don't fucking

touch her," West breathes out, his eyes flying over my face as if to check that I'm okay.

"*Pote*, let's step outside," Pierre suggests, his tone calm. And colder than I've ever heard it.

Shit. Shit. Shit.

I narrow my eyes at West. I've never seen him so keyed up and I've witnessed him lose his cool after tough losses at UCLA, then afterwards, when we couldn't make our long-distance relationship work. He struggles to check his anger but it's there, simmering under the surface, waiting for an opportunity to flare. Trying to diffuse the situation, I place a hand on his forearm. "West. What are you doing here?"

His face twists as if I slapped him. "I'm here for you, Nova. And you're...out on a date with another fucking man?" He gestures angrily toward Pierre.

"*Merde!*" The man seated behind me gasps as his wife clutches at her neck. Probably looking for some fucking pearls.

Pierre's body stiffens behind me, but he doesn't back up. Instead, he shoves at West. "Not the place, *pote*. Don't come in here, telling lies about Nova and—"

"We broke up," I remind him. "And that doesn't explain anything!" I glare at West. "I'm working, West. And you come storming in here and—"

"Working?" West bites out, his eyebrows nearly flying off his face. He gestures between Pierre and me. "Is that what you call this in France? Because—"

"Stop it," I hiss, giving him a shove. "Stop embarrassing me."

"You're doing that all on you own, babe," he claps back.

In the corner of my eye, I see Pierre gesture for the check.

We're making a spectacle. We're living up to the American stereotype. We're...fucking this up.

"Don't speak to her that way," Pierre snaps at West. He

physically lifts me up and shifts me onto the chair behind him before standing in front of me like a guardian.

Oh, no. I shudder as I feel the glacial shift take place in West. The anger from an instant ago cools to something much more dangerous. A recklessness envelops his frame. His expression locks down. His eyes lose their focus. And then, he swings. One packed, precise jab that catches Pierre off guard and snaps his head to the side.

"*Merde!*" the nearby patron exclaims again. He grasps his wife and hurries her away from our table and the exchange of blows that's now happening.

Pierre swears and swings at West who blocks him easily. Grasping for his throat, West spins and pins Pierre up against a nearby booth. He leans close, his shoulders bunching, his voice low. But I hear him spit, "Don't fucking get in between me and Nova again."

Then, West releases Pierre and I watch in horror as the kind man who has done nothing but try to defend me rubs at his throat.

West turns toward me, his expression softening as he clocks the horror in mine. "Nova."

"Don't touch me," I hiss, throwing up a hand. I move toward Pierre, desperate to know if he's okay. He waves me off, shooting me a look not to come closer.

My stomach roils and my vision grows hazy. Heat blazes on my skin as I suck in a breath. I feel unsteady. On edge. Panicked.

And then—"Police!" someone hollers in French.

I plop down in the chair, my hands gripping the underside of the table. West drops to his knees beside me, concern evident in his eyes. "Nova, what is it? What's wrong?"

I shake my head, feeling tears pool in my eyes. "How could you do this to me, West?"

"What?" He reaches for me. One hand settles on the small of my back, the other on top of my thigh.

I'm too out of it to push him away. I pull in another breath, hold it in my lungs, and slowly exhale.

Around me, it feels like my world explodes.

"Nova, talk to me!" West demands, that edge of panic now in his tone.

"You're coming with us," a police officer announces. Two officers grasp West under the arms and haul him to his feet.

"Nova!" he shouts, his eyes locked on mine. It's as if he doesn't even care that he's about to be hauled to jail.

I focus on him. Drown in the depths of his eyes. Eyes that used to make me feel safe and protected. And now, I want to lash out at him and hurt him as much as he embarrassed me.

But I can't. Because…fuck, I still care about him.

"Don't make this any worse," I snap.

His brows furrow. I look away as he's dragged through the doors and into a waiting police car.

The door slams shut and the car drives away. Silence envelops the restaurant, a heavy beat of uncertainty.

And then—"A round on me," Pierre announces, redirecting everyone's attention. "I ask, please, that you keep your videos and photos to yourselves in order to respect my date's and my privacy."

A cheer goes up as patrons nod and put their phones away, losing interest in the brawl. They resume their dinners and conversations.

"Pierre." I stand and step toward him.

"It's okay, *ma belle*," he mutters, holding a cloth napkin stained with his blood to his nose. He exchanges a few words with a nearby server, arranging to put our bill and the drinks he's now buying everyone on his tab. "Let me take you home."

"You should see a doctor," I protest.

He chuckles, even as his cheek begins to swell. "It's nothing. I've been in a bar fight before."

I bite my bottom lip. I'd hardly call that a bar fight since

West is the only one who got a punch in, but I obviously refrain from saying anything. "I'm so sorry. I don't even know what to say."

He shakes his head, his eyes studying my face. "We will talk, Nova. But not tonight."

I drop my head, feeling like I've been chastised. And worse? I deserve it.

"Are you okay?" Pierre asks as he helps me into the back seat of the car.

"I'm fine," I say robotically as a wave of exhaustion crashes over me.

Hours ago, I was trying to get myself excited to have dinner with Pierre. And I felt twinges of what I used to feel when West would pick me up and take me on a date. A little flutter of giddiness in my abdomen. A tiny thrill that danced over my shoulders. I spent time to carefully consider my outfit—a black leather miniskirt with boots and a deep red cropped cashmere sweater. Who knows how much longer I'll be able to wear crop tops before my belly swells?

I snort at the thought.

I felt wisps of excitement and then, West appeared out of thin air. West, with his flashing eyes and nasty words.

And my heart fucking galloped. My abdomen tightened. My chest burst. And I know that whatever I feel for Pierre— whatever I feel for any man—will always dull in comparison to West Crawford. That man lights up my world in a way that makes every other relationship fall flat.

And then, he made a scene, hit Pierre, and got hauled off to the French version of the drunk tank.

"I'll call you," Pierre promises as we pull up to my building.

I dip my head, wincing at the gash above his lip. I reach out gingerly and he turns away. My hand falls. "I'm so sorry, Pierre."

"Me too, Nova."

He doesn't say anything else. Shit, he won't even look at me. "Good night," I breathe out.

Then, I slide from the car, force myself to hold my head high, and take the steps up to my flat. Once I'm safely inside, I rattle off a text to the group.

> Me: West is here! He hit Pierre and got hauled off to jail.

Without waiting for any replies, I call my brother.

"Nova? You okay?" Gabe answers on the first ring.

I roll my eyes. They sting with tears. I blink rapidly to keep them from falling. At the concern in my brother's voice, I sink to the sofa and lean on Gabe for support. Right now, I need something stable to reach for.

"Nova," Gabe presses.

I sniffle.

"What happened? Where are you?" he demands.

"Home," I admit.

"Are you okay?"

"West is here."

"Yeah!" He laughs. Laughs! "Dad told me he stopped by the vineyard. He's in town to surprise you. Wait, shit, did something happen?"

What? West met Dad? Surprise me? He fucking surprised me all right.

"He showed up when I was out to dinner with Pierre," I confess.

Gabe groans, piecing together the story. "I take it he didn't react well?"

"He's in jail."

"What?" Gabe gasps, a thread of amusement in his tone. "What'd he do? Hit Pierre?"

"Yep," I confirm.

"Oh, shit!" Gabe exclaims. "You want to go get him?"

"I'm thinking about it," I admit, debating my options. It's not like I can just leave West in jail. I mean, not for longer than one night. Argh. As angry as I am with him, a part of me wants to see him. Talk to him. Be with him.

I feel sick with worry. Does he know I'm pregnant? Is that why he came? Or did he really come…for me?

"Cold-blooded, Nov," my brother says, a note of admiration in his tone. "What do you want to do?"

I sigh. "Can you take me to the police station?"

"Of course. Sit tight, my little bruiser."

"I didn't get in a bar fight."

"Nope. Just caused one," he says cheerily. "I'll see you in twenty minutes."

"Thanks, Gabe."

"Yep." He disconnects the call.

I lean back on the sofa. A suitcase in the corner of my living room catches my attention and I gape.

"You've gotta be fucking kidding me!"

I stand and stalk to the suitcase, checking the luggage tag to confirm that—yep, it belongs to West. Ugh, my father doesn't know when he should quit meddling.

A new shock of anger bolts through my system, quickly followed by a surge of helplessness. My emotions swing wildly, bringing me close to shouting and tears in the same breath.

I pull in a deep breath and try to calm my racing mind from drawing conclusions. I can't spiral now. Hell, I never spiral. I'm always cool under pressure. Maybe even funny with how easy I take things in stride.

But right now, I don't feel like myself at all.

My hands cup my lower abdomen. There isn't even a swell yet, but I know, my little one is wreaking havoc on my emotional stability.

My screen lights up with messages and I stride back to the sofa to collect my phone. Some texts are from acquaintances in Paris who must have heard of the scene I caused—seriously, they're already pinning that shit on the woman?—and are checking in.

I ignore them and open the thread with my girls.

> Ivy: What?! He's there???

> Mckenna: What happened?

> Allegra: Shit! Nova, I'm so sorry…

Me: Did you tell him?

> Allegra: Derek did… They had dinner together in Knoxville and apparently, it came out.

> Ivy: Just out of the blue?

> Allegra: I'm so sorry.

Damn. I sigh. I can't be angry with her for telling Derek. Back when West and I were together, he and I talked about everything too.

Me: He didn't say anything. About the baby…

> Allegra: Seriously?

Ivy: He just blazed into the restaurant and started swinging?

Me: Pretty much.

Me: A, did you know he was coming to Paris?

Allegra: I called your Dad two days ago. He wanted to meet West. I swear I wasn't trying to fuck with your life. I just… I wanted to help. You're carrying around a big secret and you're all alone.

Me: My family is here.

Ivy: But we're not.

Me: (sticking out tongue emoji)

Mckenna: How did your dad and brothers take the news?

I swear. More people I have to loop in.

Me: They don't know.

Ivy: You need to tell them, Nova. Get ahead of it before they find out from someone else.

Mckenna: Are you okay?

Allegra: Is West still in jail?

I roll my eyes.

Me: Relax, Gabe and I are going to get him.

Me: He could use some time to cool off.

Me: And think about his actions.

Allegra: You're going to make a wonderful mother.

Ivy: I was just thinking that! The tone, Nova— you're a natural.

Me: (middle finger emoji)

Allegra: We love you, Nova.

Mckenna: You still haven't answered—are you okay?

I drop my head back against the cushions and close my eyes.

Am I okay? Not even a little.

Me: I will be.

11

WEST

The cold metal of the bench seeps into my ass, cooling my anger. Fuck. I'm in the damn drunk tank. In France.

I gaze at my swollen knuckles. I can't believe I punched that guy.

Callie's going to lose her shit on me. I groan, wondering what my team will say. I mean, the guys have had altercations over the years, but the franchise tries to uphold the values of the brand.

Coyotes don't get into stupid fucking bar fights.

And Nova. What does she think? She must hate me.

Hell, I saw the disbelief in her expression. It's like she saw that side of me for the first time. The side *he* gifted me. Dear old dad. Quick fists, an angry tongue, and no goddamn consideration for repercussions.

I glance around my surroundings. I'm becoming just like him.

Already landing myself here, locked up and told to calm the hell down.

I heave out a sigh. I fucked up. Big time.

A jangle of keys cuts the air and I straighten, my head snapping up.

An officer comes into view, followed by Nova and, I narrow my eyes, her brother? It's definitely not the Frenchman she was dining with and that's a relief. If she showed up with him, I'd probably be put in solitary confinement.

I don't give a shit that I'm not supposed to weigh in on her life. I hated seeing that fucker's hand on her. I hated that she gave him *that* smile. The one that used to belong to me.

And then, she defended him!

"You're getting out," the officer says.

"I—" I start to ask questions.

"All taken care of, man," Nova's brother cuts me off. His voice is hard, but his eyes are more curious than angry.

I sigh. "Thank you." I step out of the jail cell, and it clangs shut behind me.

I look at Nova. "I'm so fucking sorry, Nov."

She ignores me, staring at the space on the floor between our shoes.

I flick my gaze to her brother and hold out a hand. "I'm West."

He takes my offered hand and gives it a firm shake. "Gabe. I know who you are. What I want to know is why the fuck you're here?" The challenge is low in his tone.

"I'm here for your sister," I say truthfully.

Gabe's eyes narrow as he studies me. Nova lifts her face to mine.

"Can we talk?" I ask her.

She heaves out a sigh and turns on her heel, walking down the hallway. "Maybe tomorrow, Crawford. I'm too tired to listen to your bullshit tonight."

Gabe snorts out a laugh and I try to hide my smile.

There's my feisty, fierce girl. "God, I fucking miss her."

Gabe glances at me. Then, he gives a sharp nod and follows his sister.

Trailing them, I leave my first stint in a French jail and pray it will be my last. That I won't turn into *him*. That I'll be better. Do better.

But fuck, I'm not holding my breath either.

The car is riddled with tension as I slide into the back seat.

Damn. I feel like a scolded child, banished to the back seat as the parents ride up front, their eyes focused forward, their shoulder blades squeezing.

It almost causes a smile to curve my lips. I sure as fuck never had this but—is this what my kid will feel like when he or she gets into trouble?

I glance at Nova. Study her profile. Mentally draw a line that skates over her forehead, trails down the length of her adorable nose, dips inward before flaring over the fullness of her mouth, and then, a gentle sweep over the curve of her chin before dragging down the column of her neck. She's gorgeous, even in anger. And knowing her—that sassy attitude mixed with so much damn love, and an ability to shower it on those closest to her—she's going to make one hell of a mom.

The kind of mom kids like me dream of.

"How was jail, West?" Nova snaps, spinning in her seat to glare at me.

Gabe snorts.

"Shitty," I admit, scratching my cheek.

"Are you happy with the fucking scene you caused?" She tears into me.

I glance at Gabe, meeting his eyes in the rearview mirror the same way I met Michele's earlier today. Was that only hours ago?

"Hardly," I snap back. "I'm sorry for embarrassing you, Nov. I'm even a little sorry for punching fucking Deep Pockets," I admit. "But I won't apologize for showing up here, Nova. I'm not sorry for seeing your beautiful face, even if you look like you wanna deck me."

Gabe chuckles lightly.

Nova glares.

"Where are you staying, West?" Gabe asks as we pull up to Nova's flat.

"Not here," Nova says.

At the same time, I reply, "Nova's."

Gabe's eyes flicker to mine again before he turns toward his sister.

"My suitcase is at your place," I tell her.

"I saw that," she seethes. "And I don't appreciate Dad meddling, thinking that just because you're here, you have honorable intentions."

"My intentions are always honorable when it comes to you. It's everyone else who should be wary," I say truthfully.

Gabe idles in front of the flat, his eyes trained on his sister. "It's your call," he reminds her. And I like that if Nova shuts me down, Gabe will haul my ass to a hotel. He'll do whatever his sister wants, the way a big brother should look out for her.

Will my kid have a sibling one day? Will they be tight, them against the world? I never had that either, but I've seen it. Cohen's close with his brother Cooper. Avery and Raia are buddies, bickering as frequently as they prank each other.

"Fine," Nova bites out, whirling to jab a finger in my direction. "But just tonight. Tomorrow, you can piss right off to whatever fucking hotel you want."

"The George-Louis Hotel," I say, confirming the reservation Derek made for me.

Gabe snorts and Nova arches an eyebrow. "Deep pockets," she scoffs, tossing my classification of her little friend back in my face.

I shrug, not wanting to toss Derek under the bus. I don't know shit about the hotel but I'm guessing it's fancy as fuck. The thought makes me grin for real—Derek Reiner is full of surprises.

"You sure?" Gabe asks, not bothering to keep his voice low.

Nova rolls her eyes. "It's fine." She whips around to narrow her eyes at me. "He'll be sleeping on the couch."

I hold up my hands to let her know I'm cool with whatever she decides.

Nova huffs before getting out of the car and slamming the door.

I look at Gabe. "Thanks for the ride. I appreciate it."

He nods as he turns to catch my eyes. "My dad likes you."

"I like him too. He's a great guy."

"He's the best," Gabe agrees. "But Nova makes up her own mind. Don't think you can get to her through Dad or Jacques or me. At the end of the day, we'll always back Nova."

"That's the way it should be," I agree quietly.

"Yeah." Gabe nods again. "But for what it's worth, I hope you win her back. She smiled a hell of a lot more when you were in her life. And Deep Pockets won't motivate and support her the way you did. With him, she'll be well cared for, like a pretty decoration." His jaw tightens as he mentally dismisses the thought. "She deserves more than that."

"She deserves the fucking world," I agree, before slipping out of the back seat.

I hurry to the front door where Nova is already jamming in her key, no doubt considering slamming the door in my face and forcing me to sleep outside.

I catch the door before it closes.

Nova ignores me as I follow her up the stairs to her flat. I look around, taking in the crisp paint and the iron railing. It's statelier and more traditional than the sleek, contemporary condos of Knoxville.

I follow her through the door of number five. The moment the latch catches, Nova whirls on me.

"Why are you here, West?" she spits out.

I stare at her, keeping my voice even. I want her to tell me. I want to hear her say it. "Why do you think, Nova?"

She freezes, uncertainty washing over her face. Why doesn't she want me to know? Why doesn't she trust me? Her eyes flare, then narrow. She shakes her head. "I'm not doing this right now."

I let out a hearty laugh. "So that's it? You don't want to have a conversation so—"

"You assaulted my date!" she shouts.

I laugh, even though it's not fucking funny. "I thought it was a business meeting."

She swears, shaking her head, as tears gather in her eyes.

I hate when she cries.

But also, we need to have this fight.

Because there is a massive elephant in the center of the room that neither of us is mentioning.

I shuffle back half a step. I didn't think we'd be warring tonight, and I'm not mentally equipped to spar with her. Not when I spent hours locked up, musing over my fucked-up childhood and piece of shit father. Not when I saw her smiling at another man, and she looked…happy. Not when I want to reach out, wrap her in my arms, and hold her against my chest.

Just know that she's…here. That I haven't lost her yet.

"That's what I thought," I bite out, taking her silence as confirmation.

She wipes a hand over eyes. "I'll get you a pillow and blanket." Nova gestures toward her feminine, dainty sofa, that looks like the most uncomfortable fucking couch I've ever seen.

I swear. "Look, if you really don't want me to stay, I'll go to the hotel." I move toward my suitcase, tucked into the corner of her living room.

She scoffs but her eyes soften. "It's fine. Honestly, I'm too tired to do this tonight."

Something in my chest aches at the break in her voice. "Are you okay?" I take in the exhaustion that rings her eyes, the way she nervously nibbles on her lower lip. *How are you feeling?* I want to ask. But I don't. Because she still hasn't told me about the baby. Our baby.

Nova Martin is gorgeous on a bad day. On a good day, she's fucking radiant. But tonight, she looks exhausted, and I feel awful for keeping her up, running around the city with her brother, to spring me from a damn jail cell.

"Everyone keeps asking me that," she sighs. "As if hoping the answer will be different." She gives me a small, heartbreaking smile.

"You'll be okay, Nov," I say truthfully. I know in my gut that she'll always land on her feet. She's too smart to falter when it counts.

"I'm a mess," she says, dropping her arms to her side.

"You're beautiful," I counter, my frustration from earlier seeping away now that I'm here. Finally with her.

"West, I look awful."

"Not to me."

"Yeah, well, you're color-blind anyway," she tosses out.

I snort, recalling the day I wore two different socks to dinner and Nova looked truly shocked to discover I am actually color vision deficient. Another trait inherited from my worthless father. Jesus, did he do one good thing for me?

Shit. Will my kid know his or her colors? Or will they perpetually confuse blue and green, yellow and red?

Nova walks over to a hall closet and returns a second later with a pillow and duvet. She drops them both on the sofa.

Her eyes meet mine, curious and hesitant. "Why'd you come, West?"

My throat tightens and my stomach twists at the heartache in her tone. Does she really not want me here? Did she really think I'd let her have my baby and not...do anything? Not even show up?

"Why do you think, Nova?" I flip it back on her. *Tell me about the baby!*

She doesn't.

Instead, she shakes her head. "It doesn't matter. You're here now. We'll talk tomorrow." Her voice is quiet, almost as if she's convincing herself. With that, she turns and walks toward the door that I assume leads to her bedroom.

"'Night, Nov," I mutter.

"Good night," she replies before closing her bedroom door with a snick.

I heave out a sigh. She still hasn't told me shit and yet, it's clear that she knows that I know.

How long are we going to circle around each other and let this tension tighten between us? I came to Paris for answers and I still know jack shit about my baby that's growing in Nova's belly.

On one hand, I'm glad I met her father and brother and know she has a legit support system here. On the other hand, I hate that she's...moving on with fucking Deep Pockets.

But she's right about one thing: we do need to talk.

Tomorrow. Tomorrow, we will hash it out.

Resolve settles around me. I open my suitcase, grab my Dopp kit and a pair of sweat shorts, and find a bathroom. After a hot shower—washing away a long-ass flight, an introduction with Nova's dad, a poor fucking judgement call, and the stink of a jail cell—I ready for sleep and make a bed on the sofa.

The second I sink onto it, a pillow shoved beneath my head, I groan.

It's more uncomfortable than it looks.

But it doesn't matter. I'm too tired to care about a good night's sleep.

Besides, Nova's on the other side of the wall.

For her, I'd sleep standing up.

12

Nova

THE WAVE OF NAUSEA TWISTS MY STOMACH AND CAUSES A FLUSH to wash over my body.

"Argh," I call out, trying to untangle my legs from the sheets before I face-plant on my bedroom floor. Ripping free, I rush to the bathroom, my knees hitting the tiles right before vomit and bile crawl up my throat.

I heave, emptying the contents of my stomach.

"Crap," I mutter, closing my eyes as dizziness swims in my mind.

"Nova." His voice is soft, as if he's scared to disturb me.

I groan in response.

"Shit, baby." West kneels beside me, gingerly placing a hand on my lower back. The anger I anticipate is nowhere to be found. Instead, concern wafts off him. "Tell me what you need."

"Water," I croak a second before a second stream pours from my mouth.

Seriously? I don't want West to see me like this. I don't want him to think I can't handle it. That I'm…weak. Or worse, that I need him.

I don't need anyone. I can get myself through this.

Hell, I watched my father single-handedly raise three kids after my mom passed and he did an all right job.

But when the cool washcloth hits the back of my neck and the glass of water is held to my lips, I begrudgingly admit—only to myself—that it feels nice to be cared for.

I keep my eyes closed as I sip the water. An old memory, from my childhood, flickers to life in my mind. I must have been six or seven years old. I was sick, burning up with fever, and suffering from strep throat. We were still living in America, and I was sleeping in Mom and Dad's bed except Dad was in Paris for business. Mom held my shivering body against hers, murmuring soothing sounds into my ear and brushing my hair away from my face. She held a blue cup with a silly, bendy straw to my lips and I sucked greedily.

Nice and easy, she said.

You're okay, Nova.

Tears prick the corners of my eyes.

Am I? I sure as hell don't feel okay.

"Is there more?" West asks, breaking into my memory.

I force my eyes open as I take stock of my body. The nausea has eased, and my head is less foggy. "No," I say, meeting his gaze.

The concern layered with compassion in his eyes hits me like a sucker punch.

I splay my hand against the toilet seat, ready to heave myself up when West gathers me in his arms and plucks me from the floor.

"You don't have to carry me," I protest as he stands.

"I want to," he shuts me up.

"I need to brush my teeth."

West sets me down on the vanity, stepping between my thighs to keep me steady, as he pulls my toothbrush and toothpaste from the top left drawer, the same place I kept it at my apartment in California.

"Open," he says, holding the toothbrush to my mouth.

I huff and swipe the toothbrush from him. I'll brush my own damn teeth. I brush quickly and rinse the toothpaste from my mouth.

Then, I'm back in West's arms. He carries me to my bed and gently places me in the center, fluffing my pillows and pulling the duvet up to my chin.

"If your team cuts you, you could take up nursing," I joke, keeping my voice light.

West sits on the edge of my bed. One hand rests on top of my abdomen as his eyes meet mine. Worried, caring eyes.

"So, I guess the cat's out of the bag," I announce.

West lifts his eyebrows, waiting.

I clear my throat. The big emotions—the anger and hurt—from last night died with the morning light. Instead, I just want to tell West the truth and unburden myself. "I'm pregnant, West."

"I know, Nova," he murmurs, confirming what Allegra already told me.

"You're here for the baby," I say, a part of me relieved while another part wants him to refute my statement. A part of me that I am so damn ashamed of wants him to be here for *me*. I want to know that he eventually would have come, couldn't keep staying away, because of his feelings for me. Not only because I'm pregnant with his baby.

Ugh, what kind of a mother thinks that?

"I'm here for both of you. I was waiting for you tell me," he admits.

My eyes tear. Again!

"How often does this happen?" He gestures toward the bathroom.

I sigh. "Every morning. Sometimes more."

"Fuck," he swears. "Does your dad know? Your brothers?"

I snort. "No one knows I'm pregnant, remember? I mean, just my friends, Derek, and you."

"A few of my teammates know. And Mav," he supplies.

I try to sit up but my head swims.

West's large hand flies out to push me back down. "Rest, Nova. None of them will say anything until you're ready."

"I thought you were going to out me last night. Announce it to the whole damn restaurant."

He rears back, as if I offended him. "I'd never put you on blast like that." And then, realization dawns in his eyes. "So, you've been managing on your own," he says softly.

"I don't need help." I sound defensive. My hand brushes over my lower abdomen. "I can do this."

"It never crossed my mind that you'd be anything less than the best mother any kid could wish for."

My eyes fly to his. The emotion brimming in his dark eyes nearly undoes me. He places his hand over mine.

"But if you think I won't be involved or I don't care..." West trails off, shaking his head. His hand curls, his fingers tightening on mine. "I'm here, Nova. And I'm not going anywhere. I know you don't *need* me. But did you ever think that I need you? That I need to be here for..." He pats my hand. "Whatever you need, I got you."

I let out a sigh, unsure how I feel about his declaration. On one hand, I love that he wants to be here for the baby. Deep down, I knew he'd step up and be a great father. On the other hand, can I truly trust him? And how much can I—should I—rely on him? At the end of the day, if I didn't become pregnant, West and I wouldn't be on speaking terms. We'd be broken up and he'd be—

"What's your girlfriend think about this?"

West jerks back at my tone. At my unexpected question. "Girlfriend?" His eyebrows furrow.

Jesus, is he wondering which woman I'm referring to? How many are there?

"The model," I remind him, trying to keep my voice

empty. My tone bored. Ivy clued me in when photos popped up of him and Marisa Mella at a gala in Washington DC.

West snorts. "Marisa?"

Yes! I shrug.

"That was…" He shakes his head. "That's not a thing."

I lift an eyebrow.

"You're the only woman that ever mattered, Nova. You know that," he reminds me softly. "Marisa's a PR stunt. A business contract I now need to get out of."

I sigh, not wanting his sweet words when his social media accounts, his public persona, say the opposite.

"Besides, what about…Deep Pockets?" His jaw tightens.

"Pierre," I correct.

West scoffs.

I shake my head. "He's…harmless. We have business together as he's going to start selling my family's label in two of his restaurants."

"But you like him," West presses.

I shrug. "He's a nice guy."

West looks away and I know he's trying to lock down his emotions.

I lace my fingers with his. "But no one has ever made me feel like you, West."

He meets my gaze again. Holds it. Lets out a deep exhale.

A myriad of expressions cross his face—quickly—and I can't get a read on any of them.

"We should tell your dad. Your family. Together," West murmurs, changing the subject.

I look at him and uncertainty rolls through me.

"Why haven't you told them yet?" he wonders, more curious than anything else.

"Telling Dad…"

"You think he'll be disappointed?"

I shake my head. "I think he'll be…Dad. He's the most

unflappable, supportive father a girl can have. But he had a heart attack and…"

"You're scared of how he'll react?" West guesses, trying to follow my trail-offs.

"Telling him makes it real," I whisper.

West's eyes soften and he cups my cheek. "We'll tell him together, Nova. You're not alone in this."

Tears well in my eyes and my throat burns. Ugh, why do my emotions change so quickly? I hate feeling like this, this simpering, whiny, tearful woman when I'm usually confident and witty. Sure of myself. "Aren't I?" I toss back, letting West know I'm not asking him for anything.

He brushes his thumb over my cheek, ignoring my question. "When do you want to tell him?"

I sigh. "After my ultrasound this week. It will…confirm things."

West nods slowly. "What day?"

I narrow my eyes at him. "You don't have to come."

"I know. But I want to." He's sincere. "Please, Nov. Let me?"

I stare at him, noting the seriousness in his gaze. Like I'm going to keep him from hearing his kid's heartbeat? "Friday afternoon. Two o'clock."

A slow smile spreads over his lips. "Friday at two," he confirms. Then, he leans closer and brushes his lips over my forehead.

My eyes flutter closed at the feel, at the memory. At the safe feeling West's presence always wraps me in.

"Sleep, baby," he says, stroking his hand over my hair. "I'm here."

I snuggle deeper beneath my covers. With West's murmurs in my ear and his touch in my hair, my childhood memory blends with the present. They mix together beautifully and sleep beckons. I feel warm and safe and…loved.

Then, I drop into slumber.

It's as if now that West has made a grand appearance, my body has turned traitor along with my tumultuous emotions. My morning sickness is a constant presence, my exhaustion is downright clingy, and my tears—oh my tears—make themselves known at every opportunity.

To combat my inability to control my food aversions or check my feelings, I mentally throw myself into work. Each morning, after chomping down a bite of toast and a green smoothie—apparently, West is going for baby zaddy of the year—I flip him a thanks, grab my tote bag, and hurry to the tasting cellar.

My days are spent ensuring renovations on the space aren't halted by my new predicament. And fighting the nausea that swims in my stomach and the fatigue that makes the hardwood floor look as appealing as a mattress.

West doesn't give me a hard time. But every evening, upon my return, dinner is ready. Something healthy and balanced and delicious. Over the span of five days, I note two new baby books, the arrival of prenatal vitamins, and a gift card for a manicure and pedicure.

"You're spoiling me," I accuse, holding up the gift card on Thursday night.

He grins. "I'm taking care of you."

"I never asked you to."

He shrugs. "I don't care."

I frown, glaring at him. "You can't just show up here and insert yourself into my life."

He lifts an eyebrow but amusement flashes in his eyes. He thinks this is *funny*? I cross my arms over my chest.

West does the same and leans back against the kitchen island. "Do you no longer like salmon, roasted fingerling potatoes, and kale salad?" His eyes slide to the perfectly plated dinner before snapping back to mine.

"That's not the point."

"Did you know salmon contains a lot of omega-3, B6, and B12? All of those are good for you, while you grow our baby. Not to mention the vitamins benefit our little's brain development."

I gawk at him. "I don't need—" I cut myself off as his words register in my mind.

Our little.

Tears prick the corners of my eyes and I drop my head to hide my expression. My heart beats faster and my throat tightens.

"Hey…" West's voice is soft as he steps closer. His arms encircle me, and his hands gently tug me into his embrace.

My arms automatically wrap around his waist and my fingers dig into the material of his shirt. I hold on for dear life, admitting just how scared I am.

I'm having a baby. A baby!

And I'm not prepared. I don't feel ready.

"What's going on, Nov?" West whispers.

"I'm having a baby," I sob. "And I am so damn emotional."

I feel a chuckle rumble in his chest, but he doesn't voice it. I move to pull back so I can glare at him but his hand cups the back of my head and he holds my face to his chest. "*We're* having a baby," he gently corrects. "And I love your emotions. I'm here, Nova. I'm in. Whatever you need. Whatever you want. I got you." This time, he lets me go so he can meet my eyes. "Talk to me. You've spent every day this week running out of here right after your alarm sounds. Then, you're gone all day…"

I exhale, reining in my feels. "What have you been doing all day?" I wonder. The fact that I haven't asked is attributed to my pride more than my lack of interest in his life.

"I found a gym to work out at. I'm getting set up with a trainer. Doing research." He gestures to the newest book stack. "Cooking." He smiles. "Waiting for you to talk to me."

I sigh and move toward the kitchen island. My emotions are jumbled and my thoughts are shouty. I'm not ready to… talk. Instead, I slide onto a barstool and West pushes the dinner plate in my direction, passing me utensils, before filling a glass of water.

"The appointment is tomorrow," I remind him.

"I know." He looks at me, his hands braced on the island as he leans forward. "You nervous?"

I glance up in surprise. "Are you?"

"Terrified," he admits.

A smile touches my lips even though I don't want him to see it. Then, I sigh. What the hell am I doing? He's here, isn't he? As my shoulders slump, I admit, "I'm scared, too."

"I read we should hear the heartbeat tomorrow." I hear the awe in his tone.

"Yeah," I agree. "That should be cool."

He nods. "Eat."

I take a bite of the salmon. "After the appointment, maybe this weekend, want to tell my family?"

West nods slowly, rolling his lips together. He looks at me like he knows something I don't.

Immediately, my nerves fly. "What? What's wrong?"

West snorts. "Don't be mad, okay?"

My eyes narrow.

"We're having dinner at your dad's on Saturday evening. Your brothers are coming too. And the new woman Jacques is dating—"

"Jacques's dating a new woman?" I blurt out.

West bites the side of his cheek as if to tame his smile. "I've been hanging with your brothers this week, too, Nov. They're…they're fucking awesome."

I tip my head back and groan. "I bet they like you more than me right now."

West shakes his head. "They're worried about you. But, hell, I hope they like me."

I clear my throat. I already know my family adores West. How could they not?

But I'm not ready to discuss our relationship or what co-parenting will look like. A few weeks ago, West was escorting a model around America's capital, and I was trying to envision a future in France. Now…gah, the thought of trying to sort things out feels heavy. Too exhausting for tonight's conversation. "Let's take it one day at a time, West."

Disappointment clouds his features before he masks it. He knocks his knuckles against the island. "Okay. One day at a time," he agrees. But his eyes spark with challenge and I know that look.

West isn't giving up on me. Not this time.

This time, it's me who must make a decision.

I shovel salmon into my mouth, as if that will buy me more time.

But my stomach twists and I glance down at…our little.

The clock is ticking.

13
WEST

I glance around the sterile doctor's office before my eyes settle on Nova.

She looks nervous. Her hands keep smoothing over the crinkly pink paper gown. She perches on the edge of the examination chair, refusing to lean back or relax or do anything but stare at the door.

It swings open and the doctor, a petite woman with a wide smile, enters.

Nova sits up straighter and I stand. Our nervousness is palpable, hanging in the air.

"*Bonjour!*" the doctor says, glancing at the chart. She immediately switches to English. "I'm Dr. Durand. Nova and West…" Her smile widens. "It's a pleasure to meet you."

I clear my throat and extend a hand which she shakes. "Thanks for seeing us."

Dr. Durand nods before sitting on a wheeling stool. "Tell me, Nova. How are you feeling?"

Nova relaxes slightly at the doctor's friendly tone. "Emotional. Frustrated. Tired. Nauseous. Irritable," Nova rattles off her ailments.

Dr. Durand nods and makes a few notes on her chart. "How nauseous? Are you vomiting?"

"Several times a day," I cut in before Nova can downplay how sick she's been feeling.

"Yes, that, we hope, will ease up as you enter the second trimester. Now, let's get started." The doctor asks Nova some more questions before asking her to lie back. She feels around her abdomen before turning toward an ultrasound machine. "Let's get you a due date."

I hold my breath, suddenly nervous. This is it.

I step next to Nova and she reaches for me. Our hands clasp, our eyes hold, and all the silence, the hurt, the space of the past months fall away. Disappear. It doesn't matter. Nothing does except this moment. Our little.

"Some cold gel," Dr. Durand warns before squirting blue gel on Nova's abdomen.

Nova's hand flexes in mine. I grip tighter and shuffle closer.

"And now, on the screen," the doctor says.

We turn our gazes to the monitor.

She moves the wand a few times before stopping, a smile splitting her face. "Here is your baby." She points to a black blob. She clicks buttons on the machine before nodding. "And your due date is November 3."

Nova sucks in a breath as emotion I've never felt swells behind my eyes, down my throat, and into my chest.

Nova turns toward me and I stare at her. God, she's so beautiful. Right now, with wonder ringing her irises, the sage flecks expanding in awe, I've never seen a more stunning woman.

A more radiant mother.

"Would you like to hear the heartbeat?" Dr. Durand asks.

Nova and I nod, our eyes still holding. "Yes."

A second later, the most perfect rhythm I've ever heard fills the air. Elation I've never known travels through my veins and I feel like I'm flying. Floating. The kick of adrenaline, the sheer joy, the *moment* I've only ever felt playing football envelops me now.

Tears slide down Nova's cheeks and I bend over, kissing them away. I pull back slightly and our eyes hold. Fuck it. I arc my mouth over hers and press a quick kiss to her lips.

"We're having a baby," I whisper.

She bites her bottom lip, a smile forming. "A baby," she repeats, wonder in her voice.

Dr. Durand doesn't rush us and we spend a few more moments soaking up the sound of our little's heartbeat.

"That's 155 beats per minute," Dr. Durand continues.

Alarm rocks through me and I swing my gaze to the doctor's. "Is that—"

"Perfectly normal," she assures me. "Nova, you're twelve weeks along. Next week, you will enter your second trimester. Hopefully, the symptoms you're experiencing will improve. If not, give my office a call. There are some medications we can prescribe for the nausea and vomiting. I'll see you again in about a month and then, we will schedule your twenty-week scan. At that scan, you can determine your baby's sex, if you wish."

Nova and I exchange another look.

Are we going to find out? her eyes ask.

I don't know. Do you want to? mine reply.

Are you up for being surprised? hers question.

I grin. She smiles back. And another missing piece of my life slips into place. This. This is what matters. This is the most important thing.

"Do you have any questions?" Dr. Durand asks, wiping the gel off Nova's abdomen.

Nova asks about her diet and exercise. I inquire about prenatal classes. Dr. Durand answers our questions patiently and passes us a bag filled with literature for our first pregnancy.

We leave her office armed with information, another appointment date, and grumbling bellies.

"Let's go out for lunch," I say, linking my fingers with hers.

Nova looks down at our clasped hands. "Okay." She smiles at me. "I'd like that."

"Know any good places nearby?" I wonder as we turn the corner and head in the direction of her car.

She wrinkles her nose as her eyes dart around the area. We're not in the heart of the city but there are handfuls of bistros and restaurants nearby. But it's cold and overcast—not exactly ideal for wandering around and taking in the scenery.

"Down here," Nova says, pointing down a small side street. "There's a hidden bistro that has the best French onion soup." She moans.

I lift an eyebrow and squeeze her hand. "A craving?"

She laughs. "I think so."

"Then, let's get French onion soup."

We turn the corner and tuck into the welcoming bistro. The hostess greets us, and she and Nova exchange a conversation in French before we're seated by the front window.

"How do you feel?" I ask.

She exhales. "A lot better now. Honestly, I was terrified of that appointment. Seeing the baby..." She plucks the ultrasound photo from her purse and gazes at it adoringly. "Hearing the heartbeat, it made it all real, you know?"

"Yeah," I agree, my hand closing over hers. "We're having a baby, Nova."

"We are." She smiles, placing down the ultrasound.

I pull out my phone to take a quick snap of the image. Then, I send a group message to Avery, Cohen, and Talon who I'm sure are wondering what's happening on my end.

Me: (ultrasound photo)

Me: It's really happening.

Me: Here's proof.

Knowing they're probably sleeping, I slide my phone back into my coat pocket.

"You told the team?" Nova sounds surprised.

I shrug. "Only Avery, Cohen, and Talon. They were the guys with me when Derek enlightened me."

She rolls her eyes at Derek's name. "What'd they say?"

"Nothing. Talon booked me a flight. Avery drove me home and then, to the airport."

"They're not…they don't think…" she trails off, frowning.

"Ask me." I lower my voice. "We need to talk, Nova. Tomorrow, we're telling your dad and brothers that we're expecting a child. There shouldn't be things we *can't* talk about. So, ask me."

"Let's order first." She gestures for the server and orders sparkling water, our soups, and a salad for her, a sandwich for me. Then, she looks at me. "Did your teammates think I… trapped you?"

My eyebrows pull together. "No," I say automatically.

She lifts a skeptical eyebrow.

I shrug again. "I don't know what they actually think. But I made it clear that you and I—you're the woman who got away, Nova. They know that. They know what we shared, that it was a real relationship. Not a fling or a random one-night thing. I care about you. And I know that you were just as surprised by this pregnancy as I was. So much so, you didn't even tell me." My tone hardens at the end.

"I was going to. Eventually."

I snort and shake my head. "I wish I had heard it from you."

"I know."

"You unfollowed me on social media," I point out, tossing it onto the table since we're finally *talking*.

She wrinkles her nose, her eyes holding a hint of an accusation. "You sold Tillie."

"Fuck," I snort. "I *auctioned* Tilly. And I fucking regret it. It was a stupid, drunk night."

"Not to mention, a shitty cause." There's a hint of humor in Nova's voice.

I smirk. "The shittiest. Fucking nose job."

"For a stranger," she tacks on.

We both laugh. It's not funny and yet, it is. The fact that we can joke about it eases some of the tension I've been carrying around since I landed in Paris.

"You're not really dating Marisa Mella?" she asks.

I shake my head. "It's a PR stunt. An opportunity for me to clean up my image with a more stable reputation and a chance for her to use my name to garner some press and social invitations she's after. She's a cool woman."

Nova's face falls.

"But I don't feel anything for her," I continue. "I'll let her know about us since I'm still contractually obligated to show up to some events with her." Dates rolls through my mind. "Fuck, one of them is a fashion show. In Milan."

Nova's eyes widen. "You were going to come to Europe with a model for a fake appearance?"

I swear, seeing her point. "Callie set it up. To be honest, I wasn't paying attention to much of the particulars. After you cut out of town, I didn't care about anything except drowning my hurt in alcohol and celebrating the Coyotes victory with a shit ton of partying."

Nova's quiet for a beat. "Yeah. I got that impression from your socials."

"It bothered me that you cut out that morning without saying goodbye," I admit.

Nova looks down and nods once. "I'm sorry, West." She meets my eyes and I read the apology in hers. "That was… cowardly of me. It's just, I knew it would hurt. Saying goodbye. And after the night we had, your winning…" she trails off thoughtfully. "I don't know why I ever thought it could be a clean break."

"Yeah," I snort. "Me neither."

The server drops off our soups and we pick up our spoons.

"The thing with you and the French guy… What's that about? For real."

Nova winces as she burns her lip on the hot soup. She places down her spoon.

"Pierre is…a nice guy," she says slowly.

I scoff, letting my spoon clatter to the table as well.

"He's successful. Stable," she continues. "And—"

"He wants in your pants."

She narrows her eyes. "Probably no more than Marisa Mella wants in yours."

Shit. I grip the damn spoon again. We're getting off topic.

"We're having a baby," I say quietly. "There's no room for this type of jealousy. We need to work together."

"Just because we're having a baby doesn't mean we should be together, West."

My neck snaps up. My knuckles pop on the spoon. Anger flames low in my gut.

And I see red. What the fuck is she talking about?

"We can co-parent," Nova continues as if my body isn't about to combust in horror. In anger. In fucking hurt. "Having a baby doesn't automatically mean we're a good fit or—"

"What if we are?" I cut her off.

Her expression softens at the determination in my voice. "We tried and it didn't work. Nothing's changed, West."

I lift my eyebrows. "Everything's changed, Nova. You're carrying my kid."

Disappointment flickers through her eyes and I lean closer. What is she upset about?

"And if I wasn't?" she murmurs. "Would you still want me then?"

Is she serious? "Fuck yeah. I never didn't want you, Nova. I've always wanted this"—I gesture between us—"to work. You're the only woman I've ever wanted a future with. You know that. But I did a shitty job of balancing football and the distance and you. I won't make that mistake again."

Her eyes shimmer with unshed tears and I feel fucking awful for making her cry. "West."

"Don't cry, baby," I mutter, brushing my thumb over her cheek. "I want us to give this a chance, Nova. A real shot. And yeah, maybe this pregnancy is changing the situation. But not my feelings. Trust me when I tell you, I was going to find my way back to you, Nov. I don't know when or how. But me and you? We were always going to be unfinished business; I told your dad as much. Because there's never been anyone but you."

She blinks and a tear falls. I wipe it away.

"Give me a shot," I murmur. "Another chance. Please."

"What if we mess it up?" she asks. Her eyes plead with mine to understand.

"I get your hesitation," I admit. "We have a baby to think about now." I place a hand on her thigh and squeeze. "But that makes this even more important. We're a family, Nova. We always will be."

She releases an exhale and it rattles in the air between us. "I'm scared to trust this, West. The last few months, I started building a life here. One I'm proud of."

"You should be."

"I don't want to give all that up to follow you again and then…what if we don't work out? Then, I'm on my own, with a child and—"

"Do you honestly think I'd ever *not* look after you and our child—regardless of our relationship status?" I bark out, horrified.

She sighs. "No, but… I don't want to lose myself. I don't want to give up all the pieces I'm finding just because we're having a baby, and you live in Knoxville."

My heart fucking breaks at the agony in her voice. "You won't," I swear, shaking my head. "And I'm not asking you to."

"Yet," she whispers. Her eyes meet mine. "But your career is established, West. I'm still finding my footing but… I like what I'm doing here. I like my work. I just…" She heaves out another sigh. "This is a lot and things are changing so quickly."

"Things are changing," I agree. Leaning closer, I press a kiss to her temple. "But we can figure them out together. If you want to. If you let me in. Please, try with me, Nova."

She holds my eyes for a long moment. "Okay. Yes," she agrees, turning her face to mine. Her hand reaches up to cup my cheek. Her beautiful eyes hold mine. "We're having a baby, West."

I smile. "We're having a baby. And I hope he or she is just like their mama."

"Really?" Nova tilts her head. "I hope they have your mouth."

I snort. "Your eyes."

"Your athletic prowess."

I shake my head. "Your heart." I place a hand on her chest. My eyes study hers before dropping down to her mouth.

Desperate to kiss her, I meet her gaze again. I note the longing in hers. And…fuck it.

Dropping my lips to hers, I kiss her slowly. Deeply. Completely.

I don't give a shit that we're seated in front of a large window in a bistro. I don't care who sees us or gawks as they pass. I don't care about anything except Nova and our little.

Hope rolls through my veins, filling me with a lightness I

haven't felt in months. Finally, my priorities are in the right order, and I won't shuffle them again.

I won't risk losing the chance Nova is gifting me.

DAD'S HOUSE—THE FAMILIAR SCENT, THE GROOVES IN THE hardwood floors my feet know by memory, the full-bodied glass of red wine in hand—wraps around me like a hug. It feels good to be home and even better to have all my favorite guys under the same roof.

I grin as Gabe says something that makes Dad laugh in the kitchen.

"I'll take that," West whispers, plucking the glass from my hand and taking a sip. "What are you going to do? Carry it around the entire time."

"I was looking for a place to leave it," I hiss back, taking it from his hand and placing it on an end table in the living room where it's hidden behind a lamp.

West snorts, I grin, and we share a secret look.

He places a hand on my lower back, and I lean into it. God, I've missed him. I've missed *this*. The familiarity, the trust, the contentment of just being in the same space together, drawing in the same breaths. It's like we're back. The two of us, lost in our own world, a hidden universe no one else knows about. "How do you feel?" he murmurs, a line puckering between his brows.

"Good," I reply. "I feel really good today."

Relief colors his eyes. "Good. You ready to tell them?"

I nod. "I'm ready." And I am. With West by my side, I feel stronger. More stable. More equipped to grow into a mother and birth a baby.

It's not that our months apart are forgotten, it's more that I know what it's like to be without him. And I don't want to be anymore. In fact, I never wanted that.

While it's clear that my pregnancy brought us back together, West was right. We're the ones who choose to make this work. And now, we both know exactly what's at stake. What we would lose. Because we've already lived it.

"Stop canoodling in the living room and get in here," Jacques calls out, gesturing for West and me to enter the kitchen. His arm is wrapped around the woman he's been dating—for two whole months now—named Haley.

"Like you're one to talk." I point at him.

Haley blushes and Jacques shakes his head, giving me a warning look. "I'm in the kitchen with the rest of our family," he tosses back.

I stick my tongue out at him.

"You're just salty because you learned about Haley from West," Gabe says.

Haley blushes a deeper shade of red.

"Facts," West agrees, pounding fists with Gabe.

I roll my eyes and give Haley a genuine smile to make her feel better. This has nothing to do with her and everything to do with my brother who didn't even tell me he was dating!

West laces his fingers with mine and gives two quick squeezes to get my mind back on track. Moving deeper into the kitchen, I tuck our joined hands behind my back. "West and I have news."

Jacques and Gabe exchange a look. Haley looks on expectantly. Dad tries to hide his smile.

"Really?" Dad asks, crossing his arms. "What is it?"

He shoots Gabe a wink and I bite the corner of my mouth to contain my laughter.

They think they know. They think I'm going to announce that West and I are back together. Or, maybe, that I'm moving to Tennessee for next football season.

They aren't expecting the news I'm about to drop in their laps. They're not ready for the surprise blow we're going to deliver.

I roll my lips together, keeping West's and my secret, our little, close to the chest for one more heartbeat. And then, I glance at West, and he drops my hand to wrap his arm around my waist. He gives me a small nod.

"West and I are having a baby," I announce. "I'm pregnant."

Dad, Gabe, and Jacques stare at us.

Haley claps loudly, a grin breaking out on her face. "Congratulations!"

Dad's expression is pure shock. Gabe's mouth is wide open. And Jacques's eyes are narrowed.

"Don't joke about shit like that," Gabe speaks first.

Haley stops clapping, glancing around the room nervously. Her arms fall to her sides, and I feel bad for her. This sure is some way to meet the family.

"She's not joking. We're…" West glances down at me and smiles softly. "We're having a baby. Nova's due date is November 3."

"Ah, what?" Dad sputters.

"November?" Jacques questions. "So that means…" His eyes dart between us.

"You're going to be a grandpa!" I tell Dad, doing jazz fingers. "And you two can fight over who gets to be the funcle."

"What the fuck is a funcle?" Jacques mutters.

"Fun uncle," Haley whispers.

Gabe raises his hand. "Obviously, that will be me."

"You're serious," Dad says, catching on. He slips from his barstool and walks toward us.

Beside me, West straightens, as if nervous of Dad's reaction.

But I know my father.

His arms open and I fall into them. He embraces me, murmuring questions the entire time. "How are you? How do you feel? Do you need anything?"

I cling to my dad. He's always showed up for me, never wavered, and is a constant sounding board. He's the man I measure any of the guys I date against and even though I was originally salty when I learned West visited him, a larger part of me was relieved.

Grateful even.

"I'm okay. The nausea and morning sickness was rough but it's easing up now. I'm nearly in my second trimester. And now, with West here, I'm doing much better," I admit honestly.

I pull away from Dad to gauge his reaction.

Tears stream down his cheeks as he looks at me with wonder in his eyes. "I'm going to be a grandpa."

"He or she will call you grand-père," I promise.

He snorts, a laugh curling his mouth. "Grand-père," he murmurs, stunned.

Turning toward West, Dad holds out his hand. "Congratulations are in order, son."

Son. Dad's officially bringing West into the family fold, whether we're together or not.

West is quiet for a long moment and uncertainty shoots through me. Turning, I look at him, wanting to nudge him into accepting my father's offered hand. But the naked emotion I see in West's face, the disbelief I read in his eyes, gives me pause.

He's never had a family before. He's never truly belonged

to one the way most of us take our parents and siblings for granted.

West clears his throat and I hold my breath.

"Thank you, Claude," West says, shaking Dad's hand before Dad pulls him into a hug. West clasps Dad's shoulder, hugging him for real and my eyes well with tears.

"Shit, she really is emotional," Gabe mutters, as if he's just accepting my pregnancy announcement.

"You have no idea," I admit.

"That's normal," Haley offers.

Gabe smirks as Jacques gives me a searching look.

"You sure you're okay, Nov?" Jacques's eyes dart to West and back again. "With everything."

I nod at the question he didn't voice.

Am I okay being back together with West? Is that what I truly want?

"I'm more than okay," I admit. "I'm really, truly happy."

Jacques smiles and pulls me into a tight hug. "Happy for you, then."

"Me too," Gabe says, wrapping his arms around both of us.

"Jesus, your family shit is intense," West mutters.

"I'm new here," Haley chimes in as Jacques brings her into the group.

My brothers and I laugh. Then, Gabe reaches out and pulls West and Dad into the group hug.

It's corny. And silly. And so us.

It's something I used to take for granted but now, with my little growing in my belly and West's presence wrapping around me, I know better. Family is everything.

And I have the best.

"Nova, we're home," West whispers.

"Hmm?" I ask, fluttering my eyes awake.

"Come, baby," he says, scooping me into his arms.

"I can walk." I yawn.

"I know. But I can carry you too," he replies, taking the stairs like he's carrying a bag of groceries instead of his pregnant girlfriend.

West manages to get the door unlocked as I hang in his arms like deadweight. But, God, am I tired.

After announcing our pregnancy, Dad popped the cork on one of his best bottles of champagne. He, my brothers, Haley, and West toasted our happy news while I sipped on a glass of sparkling water with lemon. The mood was extremely celebratory.

Dad and my brothers asked a slew of questions which I did my best to answer. When I wasn't sure—like where are we planning to live and raise our baby?—West smoothly cut in and redirected the conversation.

"Sleep, Nova," West croons as he lays me down on the bed. His fingers make quick work of pulling off my boots. Then, he tugs my pants off my legs. His palm slides over my ass, giving it a little squeeze, before he pulls back the comforter and helps me settle underneath.

"You okay to sleep in this sweater?" His voice is soft as he pushes my hair behind my ear.

I shake my head and manage to sit halfway up and lift my arms. West tugs the sweater off my head and drops it on the end of the bed. He's quiet and I meet his eyes.

But his gaze is focused on...me. Hunger darkens his irises as he drinks me in, like he hasn't seen me in months. Except, he hasn't. And we're having a child. The realization is bizarre.

"West," I murmur, my voice hoarse with sleep and... desire.

His eyes snap to mine. Embarrassment at being caught

checking me out filters over his expression. "Sleep," he repeats. "You're tired."

I shake my head. "Not anymore." I bite my bottom lip, trying to voice my feelings. The want. The hope. The happiness.

Joy mixes with desire. Excitement thrums with lust.

And it's been so long. Nearly three months. It's been too long.

"Nova," West growls, his eyes dropping to my chest then flying back to my face. "Baby, I'm out of my depth here. Tell me… Nov, tell me exactly what you want."

"What I always want," I admit in the quiet of the bedroom. Moonlight filters in through the window but other than that, it's dark. Easier to admit the truth. "You, West. I want *you*."

He groans softly. His hand reaches out, cups my cheek, and brushes along the side of my neck. "I don't want to hurt you."

I frown. "Why would you—"

"The baby," he admits, looking down. His hand follows and his fingers swipe over my bare stomach, lingering above the waistband of my panties.

I smile. God, I love him. Haven't I always?

"The baby's fine," I promise, placing my hand over his. His palm flattens along my lower abdomen.

Leaning back against the pillow, I pull him with me. "I'm fine," I continue. "We're… Everything is good, West."

He hovers over me. His eyes dart between my eyes and my mouth as he hesitates. "Nova." My name is a plea on his lips.

"Kiss me, West."

"I won't want to stop." His eyes bleed with apology, with torture.

"I'm not going to ask you to." My voice drips with promise.

A war wages in West's eyes.

"You're not going to hurt me," I whisper, drawing him closer. "You're not going to hurt the baby."

"The things I feel for you…" he trails off, his tone practically a growl. Laced with want. Heavy with need.

"Show me," I beg, bringing his hand to my breast.

West groans, as his palm cups my right breast. He flicks his thumb over the lace covering my nipple and I whimper.

"Everything…it's so much more sensitive," I admit.

West holds my eyes for one more beat. At my encouraging nod, he lowers his mouth to my breast, pushes down the cup of my bra, and gently flicks his tongue over my nipple.

I nearly see stars as pleasure rocks through me.

"Fuck," he swears. "You're so beautiful, Nov." His palm slides over my ribs and down to my waist as he settles his frame over mine. My knees fall apart, and my thighs widen as West lays between them.

Then, his tongue darts out again. He licks my nipple before gently sucking my breast into his mouth and laving it with attention. Then, he gives my left breast the same consideration.

Heat pools between my thighs and I know I'm already wet for him. Deliriously so. Nothing has ever felt this good.

It's like my nerve endings are on fire and the feel of West's mouth, or touch, sates the burn as much as it intensifies it. He kisses the space between my breasts as my fingers thread through his hair.

"I missed this," he murmurs.

"Hooking up with me?" I joke.

West snorts. "Exploring your body. Stealing time in the darkness of night. Just, you. Fuck, I missed you, Nova."

"Me too."

"I know, baby." Then, his mouth trails down the center of my stomach. His kiss lingers on the space below my belly button, as if he's kissing our little. And then, he's rolling my panties down my thighs. His fingers part me and I moan.

"Christ, you're soaked."

"Dripping," I groan.

"So sexy." West swears, dragging his fingers through my folds again. "So responsive."

"For you," I swear.

"Only for me," he growls, his tone sharp.

And then, his mouth is between my thighs. The heat of his exhale nearly sends me over the edge. It's been too long. And everything feels so damn good.

West's thumbs part me as his tongue drags up my core.

"West." I buck off the bed.

He does it again. "Let me love you, Nova," he whispers, pressing a kiss to my clit. I fist his curls in my hand.

He smirks. Then, he flattens his tongue and gets to work on loving me. He drags his tongue through my folds, gently sucks on my clit, and nibbles along my inner thighs. He inserts one finger into my channel and my eyes nearly roll back. But then, West adds another finger. His thumb brushes along the tiny bud of nerves as his fingers slide in and out. He adds the heat of his tongue to the pressure of his touch, and I cry out, my heels digging into the mattress.

"Fuck, Nova. Look at you," he moans.

He devours me, groaning with pleasure, swearing with want, until the pressure becomes deliciously unbearable.

"West." My thighs begin to shake as I reach the peak.

"Come for me, baby," he demands, sucking on my clit.

I break. Shatter. Come apart at the seams. The wave of pleasure that rocks through me is stronger than a riptide and I ride the wave, cresting and coasting as my body quakes. West doesn't stop the ministrations of his mouth, the rhythm of his fingers. Instead, he keeps going, wringing the last drop of my orgasm from my body.

"West," I repeat. "West." It's practically a chant. But I don't know what I'm asking for. The only thing I need is *him*.

"You're incredible, Nov." He kisses me.

I kiss him back, tasting myself on his swollen lips.

"Please," I whimper.

"Tell me."

"You. I need you, West."

His eyes widen even as his hard length brushes against my inner thigh. He's rock hard and…wanting me. "Are you sure?"

I nearly laugh. "Yes. Please, don't make me beg. Just…get inside me."

"I'm clean, Nova."

I roll my eyes. "And I'm already pregnant."

West chuckles. But then, the head of his cock nudges my opening and his laughter fades. "I love you, Nova."

"I love you, too," I swear as he pushes into me, stretching my walls.

"Christ, you feel like heaven," he grunts out.

He holds still as I adjust to him.

"We still fit together perfectly," I murmur, hooking my legs around his waist.

"You're it for me. Always were," he declares as he begins to move.

West sets a pace that's perfectly languid. We linger in a space between want and need. Savoring. Sipping. Tasting. We kiss passionately, touch desperately, and love each other openly.

It's the most honest exchange of my life and I drown in it. In him.

Our lovemaking turns heated as West slowly increases the pace. I lift my hips to keep up, meeting him thrust for thrust, as a new wave of pleasure begins to build.

"More," I moan, my fingernails digging into his back.

He rocks into me. The long and deep turns short and fast until he's fucking me frantically, chasing his release.

"Fuck, baby. I'm gonna—"

"Come," I urge. "Come for me, West. Show me how much you—" I break off as I shatter a second time. My eyes close as my back arches off the mattress and presses into him.

"Nova!" He swears, releasing inside me as he collapses forward. His arms wrap around me as he falls to his side, turning until I'm splayed across his chest. His cock is still buried to the hilt, and I feel his cum leak out, slip over my inner thighs, as he slowly pulls out.

"Shit," he swears, recognizing the mess we made.

I kiss him in response and feel his mouth curve into a smile against mine. "I love you," I tell him again.

He grips my hair and holds my face, staring deeply into my eyes. "You're my family now, Nova."

"Forever," I promise.

We lay in the quiet for several heartbeats and I memorize the moment. It's one I never want to forget. After months of searching, it feels like a homecoming I didn't know I needed.

Then, we take a hot shower, strip the sheets off my bed, and remake it. When we slide underneath the covers, I reach for him, and he curls his body around mine.

We fall asleep with our limbs intertwined, our little nestled safely between us.

15

WEST

Avery: Man, this image scared the shit out of me.

Cohen: Thought it was yours?

Avery: That's not fucking funny.

Talon: (laughing emoji, skull emoji) Yeah, it is.

Avery: (middle finger emoji)

Cohen: Take it as a warning…

Avery: Fuck off.

Talon: Wrap your shit, bro.

Avery: You got sacked, Crawford.

Cohen: When's the due date?

Me: November 3.

Talon: Your kid already looks like you, Crawford.

Me: Can't kill my buzz, Tal.

Talon: Good for you, bro. Congrats???

Me: !!!

Talon: Cool. Congratulations to you both.

Me: Thanks.

Cohen: How's Nova feeling?

Me: Better. She's officially in the second trimester.

Avery: You're taking this much better than expected.

Cohen: Is he? You're acting exactly like how I'd expect, West. Avery on the other hand…

Talon: Double wrap that shit.

Avery: Happy for you, West.

Cohen: We'll celebrate when you're back in town. Enjoy time with your girl.

Me: Thanks, guys! It's been…a wild ride. But wonderful.

Talon: Christ, he already sounds like a…dad.

Me: Can't kill my vibe.

Cohen: Good for you, man!

I TOSS MY PHONE DOWN AND GAZE AT A SLEEPING NOVA. WHILE her morning sickness has subsided, she's still exhausted. Besides, telling her family emotionally drained her. While Claude, Gabe, and Jacques's reactions were positive—in fact, a hell of a lot better than I anticipated—I know it weighed on Nova's mind.

My girl needs rest. And I need…shit, I need to get the hell out of my contract with Marisa. I can't have a fashion model fake girlfriend when I have a very real pregnant one I'm desperate to plan a future with.

I pick my phone back up and leave a voicemail for Callie. Now that Nova's family knows, I'm comfortable looping in my agent. I need her on my side to navigate whatever comes next from my public fallout with Marisa.

But first, breakfast for Nova.

Relocating to the kitchen, I make Nova and me omelets for breakfast and am just pouring her coffee when she makes her way into the space, brushing her hair out of her face.

"Good morning, babe," I say, pressing a kiss to her temple and passing her the steaming mug.

"Morning." She yawns, snuggling against my chest. She holds the mug by its handle and raises it to her lips, taking a slow sip. "Mm, it's decaf, isn't it?"

I snort. "Yep. Doc said only one coffee a day and I figured you'd want to save it for the afternoon, when the exhaustion ramps up?"

She yawns again. "You'd be right." She smiles at me. "But the exhaustion is already here. Someone kept me up last night."

I grin, recalling last night. Fuck, it was perfect. Coming together with Nova was like coming home and I take a moment to mentally savor the way she looked when I pushed inside her. Her eyes lust filled and at half-mast, her breasts full and inviting, the way her hips bucked up to meet my thrusts, and her moans that—

"Stop!" she calls me out, giggling. "I know exactly what you're thinking by that expression." She points at my face.

I laugh but acquiesce, releasing her to grab our breakfast plates. "What have you got going on today?"

Nova slides into a chair at the kitchen table. "Thank you for this." She gestures to the plate I put down in front of her.

"I'm just glad you're keeping food down," I joke.

"Me too," she agrees, taking another sip of coffee. "Today,

I'm checking on the renovation progress for the tasting room. It should be done in the next two weeks."

"That's great, Nov. I can't wait to see the finished space."

"Me too. Then, I'm going to have lunch with Dad. He's coming into the city since Debbie is taking him to the doctor this morning. Routine appointment."

"You guys really never run out of things to talk about, do you?" I wonder. We just saw her father yesterday and while I love how close they are, I don't understand it.

I thought those type of relationships only existed in movies until I saw how often a few of my teammates at UCLA called their parents. How their parents drove or even flew to watch them play. And now, I see it with Avery Callaway and Cohen Campbell. Their families are tight.

"We don't," Nova agrees, patting her lower abdomen. "You'll see one day soon, West."

The thought pulls me up short and I gawk at her. Nova laughs. But she's right. Soon, I'll be a dad. God, I hope my kid wants to talk to me every day. Wants to be with me. Fucking likes me.

Will they?

I take a big gulp of coffee.

"What are you doing today?" Nova asks, continuing to eat.

"Hitting the gym. I'm trying to schedule a call with Callie."

"For an endorsement deal?"

"That too. I hope." I heave out a sigh. Not looking forward to this part. "You know how I'm...fake dating...Marisa Mella?"

Nova's grip tightens on her fork before she lets it clatter to her plate. She meets my eyes slowly, her expression locked down. "Yes." Her tone is tight, and I feel it pinch, twisting my skin. She's nervous, waiting for the other shoe to drop.

But, "I gotta get out of that."

Relief floods her features. "Oh. So, you're calling it off?"

I frown as her reaction confirms my suspicions. "Of course, I'm fucking calling it off. Nova, did you seriously think—"

"I'm not trying to argue with you, West." Nova holds up a hand. "I just," she sighs heavily, "I got nervous. That you were going to have to keep seeing her or fulfill terms of the contract or…" She shrugs.

She breaks my fucking heart.

"Nova, I don't give a fuck about Marisa Mella. Or a damn contract. All I care about is you and our little. Now, I want to loop Callie in to navigate shit with the least amount of blowback. To be honest, I don't even know what the terms are. I wasn't paying much attention when I signed shit because I didn't care. But now, it matters. You, this, it matters." I grip her hand and hang on tight.

She flips her hand and clutches my fingers. "For me too, West. I'm sorry."

"Don't be. I get why you got worried. We've…gotta find our footing again. Learn to trust each other, and our relationship, again."

"Yeah," she says softly. "I'll be home early."

I smirk. "Want to go out for dinner?"

Things between Nova and me are going so well. We're connecting again, sliding back into our old norm. But, like her, I still don't trust it. I mean, I was fully invested the first time around and look how that ended? With both of us heartbroken and lovesick.

This time, we have to get it right.

Nova looks at me for a long moment. The sage in her eyes lights and her expression is soft and sweet. God, I love her. "Yes, West. I'd love to do dinner tonight."

I smile. "Good. It's a date."

She beams back. "It's a date."

Some of the tension of her thinking I'd keep dating my

fake girlfriend subsides. I'm getting out of that contract as soon as possible and moving forward. Nova and our baby are my future. Tonight, I'm taking my woman out on a date and we're…taking the next step toward that future.

I wash up the plates as Nova gets ready for work. When she breezes past, in wide-legged trousers, a simple cream sweater, and boots, I stop to plant a kiss on her lips. "You look beautiful."

"You have to tell me that."

I laugh. "You are beautiful."

She smiles and kisses me one more time. "See you tonight?"

"See you tonight," I agree, watching her leave for work.

Then, I head to the gym, get in a hard workout, and take a shower. I'm drinking a protein shake when Callie FaceTimes.

"Hey, Cal," I answer.

"Hi!" She waves.

"How's it going?"

Callie grins. "You're going to like what I've got to tell you, Crawford." She outlines two endorsement deals that have come my way. One for an energy drink company and one for one of my favorite athletic clothing brands, Green Moose Athletics.

"No way!" My eyes widen as she tells me about Green Moose. "I love their stuff."

"I know; *they* know." She nods.

"That's sweet!" The offer is good too. A solid monetary injection I can use, especially now that I have a baby on the way.

"They want to do the photoshoot with Marisa representing their women's line as well. They loved that the two of you are *dating*," she emphasizes the word in a way that makes my stomach twist.

Shit. I need to change that ASAP.

"Callie, we're not—"

"And they can squeeze in the shoot next month. In fact, it lines up when Marisa's in Milan for the Hansen Cross show," Callie finishes.

Fuck. I close my eyes and drop my head back.

"West?" Cal asks.

I bring my head up to face her.

Whatever she reads in my expression has her eyes flaring, trepidation filling her face. "What's going on?" she demands more than asks.

I let out an exhale. "Don't freak out, okay?"

"Shit, Crawford," she moans. "Just tell me—DUI? A night in lockup? Did you sleep with—"

"I'm having a baby," I announce. While I probably should have looped Callie in sooner, I didn't want to tell her, or anyone other than the teammates who already knew, until Nova and I were on solid footing.

And we are now. We're dating. Her family knows. We're... taking the next step. Damn, we're taking a quantum leap.

Callie sighs. Swallows. Nods. Clears her throat. "Okay. How much is she—"

"No," I cut her off before she can finish the sentence. "Don't finish that thought. It's Nova. It's... Callie, it's why I'm in Paris. I can't date Marisa Mella, fake or not. I'm...fuck, I'm trying to get my girl back, Cal."

Her eyebrows furrow and a little line draws between them. "You're...happy?"

I bark out a laugh. And then, realize I am. Happy. Christ, is that what this feeling is? It's been so long since I've felt so... light. Excited. Fucking hopeful. "Yeah, Cal. I'm fucking...shit, I'm happier than I've been in a long time," I admit.

She stares at me for a beat before a smile spreads across her face. "Good for you, West. If you're happy, and I can tell you are, then I'm happy for you. A baby is always a blessing," she tacks on softly.

At the emotion in her tone, I suck in a breath to keep my

feelings locked down. I can't get sentimental with my agent. Not when I need her to get me out of this contract with Marisa and still ensure I get the endorsement deal. We have serious topics to discuss, decisions to make.

Instead, "What color would you paint a nursery?" tumbles out of my fucking mouth, surprising us both.

Surprise flares in her eyes before she replies, "Do you know the sex?"

"No." I shake my head.

"Are you going to find out?"

A bubble of excitement expands in my stomach. "Nope. We're going to be surprised."

Callie chuckles. "Okay, so, we're doing this, Crawford? Having this conversation?" she asks, a hint of hesitation.

I laugh. "Seems like it, Cal."

"Well, I'd talk to Nova first."

"I'm trying to surprise her. Take something off her plate," I explain. "She has so much going on with work, and is in the middle of a reno. If I can set up the nursery, I think she'd like that."

Callie's eyes widen and the corners of her lips turn up. "You love her."

It's a statement. A fucking fact.

"I've always loved her."

"That's why you were partying it up, doing stupid shit in Vegas," Callie continues, putting the pieces together. "You were trying to..."

"It didn't work. Nova's not a woman you move on from."

Callie nods. "I get that now." She studies me for a long beat. Then, in a softer tone, she murmurs, "Manchester Tan, Calm, or Cloud White for colors. I think a nice, sage green or soft, creamy yellow would look nice as accents, too."

Sage green. Like the flecks in Nova's eyes.

I clear my throat. "Thanks, Callie. That sounds good. I'll check those colors out."

She nods slowly. "You need to get out of your contract with Marisa."

"As soon as possible."

Callie sighs. "I'll see what I can do, West. But the Hansen Cross show is next month and…"

"I don't care, Cal. Whatever it takes, I want out."

"Okay. But she still may have the endorsement option. It won't have to be marketed as y'all dating but—"

"That's fine." I wave a hand. I can't undercut Marisa's professional opportunities. We can work together, as long as the public doesn't think we are together.

Callie grins, surprising me as I thought she'd be miffed. "Happiness looks good on you, West. I'll circle back soon, after I sort things out on my end."

"Thanks, Callie. I appreciate you."

She snorts. "You better."

I say goodbye and disconnect the call. Then, I grab my laptop and begin my important research.

Paint colors.

Nursery design.

Reviews on baby products.

The things that truly matter.

16

Nova

"You made reservations," I sound surprised as West parks my car near a new, trendy restaurant in the 6th arrondissement, close to the Luxembourg Gardens.

"I did," West sounds proud.

I stifle a laugh, knowing he must have done some research—even if the bulk of it entailed calling one of my brothers—to settle on a restaurant for tonight.

West looks delicious, dressed in dark jeans, a midnight grey, V-neck T-shirt, and a charcoal, linen blend blazer. He's wearing loafers, has a colorful pop of color tucked into his pocket, and got a haircut.

I bite my bottom lip. "Paris looks good on you, West." I gesture toward his look as I close the passenger door.

He smirks. "Callie said something similar today." He takes my hand, squeezes it twice, and brings the back of it to his mouth, placing a kiss there. "I actually went shopping. Your brother took me."

"I see that." My eyes widen. West hates shopping. But the fact that he let Gabe drag him to different stores to buy an outfit speaks volumes.

He grins, but his eyes darken. "You look stunning, Nova." He shakes his head. "That dress... When you turned around," he sighs. "So goddamn sexy; I can't believe I'm taking you to dinner when there are other things we could be doing."

"Afterwards." I beam, loving that my dress affects him.

I'm wearing a little black dress that I adore. It's simple enough from the front, but the back is open with a massive bow that ties behind my neck, the ribbons floating to the small of my back. I paired it with sheer, black tights, and black pumps.

With my hand in his, we walk to the restaurant.

"Oh! I've been wanting to go here!" I exclaim as the door opens for us.

"I heard," West says cryptically.

"Jacques or Gabe?"

"Jacques," West offers. "He took Haley here to seal the deal."

I snort. "Is that what you're doing? Sealing the deal?"

"Baby, I thought I did that last night?"

I smirk and greet the hostess. West gives his name and we're quickly led to a prime table in the center of the space.

"This place is booked solid for weeks. How'd you get a reservation?" I ask as I take a seat.

West lifts an eyebrow. "Seriously?" He drolls. "I know football doesn't mean much here but...I did win a Super Bowl."

I snort. "You know people?"

"Avery slept with a French singer last year," he grumbles.

I tip my head back and laugh. "So, Avery knows people?"

West quirks an eyebrow but he's grinning. "And I know Avery."

"Touchè." I point at him.

"Wine?" the waiter asks, appearing at our table.

I'm about to ask for a wine list for West when he shakes his head.

"No, thank you," I decline, switching to French to explain that I'm expecting and joke that West is abstaining from alcohol in solidarity. The waiter looks bewildered but says he will be back in a moment with the sparkling water I order us.

Once he leaves, West smiles at me. "Will you teach our baby French?"

"*Oui*," I reply.

His grin grows. "That's good. I always wanted to learn a second language."

"It's not too late."

He scoffs. "School was never my thing."

Sometimes, it breaks my heart that West never had the loving family or supportive school experiences I did. He sells himself short regularly and doesn't see how amazing he is, even more so because of the challenges he overcame.

"You didn't get a fair shot," I remind him.

He shrugs.

"Our baby is lucky," I say, leaning closer.

"With you as a mama? Yeah, our little hit the lottery."

"Thanks. But I was going to say having you as a dad. You don't see it, West, but your heart—"

"Nov," he interjects.

I speak over him. "Is big. You love hard. You're loyal and fair and driven. You didn't get a fair shot but that doesn't mean you don't know how to give one."

He's quiet as I arch an eyebrow, daring him to contradict me.

West clears his throat. "You really think I can do it? Be a good dad?"

My chest twists at the hesitant expression on his face, at the hope in his eyes. I nod. "You already are, West."

He breathes out a shaky exhale.

Our waiter reappears and we order.

Then, I spend the evening reconnecting with the first and only man I ever loved. The one I hope will also be the last.

My always.

Sleeping in West's arms, with his legs entangled with mine, his cheek pressed next to my hair, his scent enveloping me, steadies me. His presence centers me and helps me find my footing again.

So much so, that when my brothers stop by the tasting room a few days later and ask if I can spend a week at the vineyard, looking after Dad, I say yes.

"Are you sure you'll be okay on your own?" Jacques inquires. "Deb won't be there. She's on holiday."

"Well deserved and good for Debbie," I counter.

"I know you haven't felt one hundred percent either—" Gabe starts.

"I'm doing much better, guys. Honestly." I fold my arms across my chest. "I'm worried about Dad. Why do you think one of us should stay there?"

Jacques sighs and pinches the bridge of his nose. He shoots Gabe a look.

"What is it? What's wrong?" I jump to the worst-case scenario, my mind conjuring up a variety of diagnoses in a heartbeat.

"Nothing!" Gabe rushes out. "Dad's just been tired lately. He had his checkup at the doctor and his blood work isn't ideal. I think he needs the extra support and with Debbie on holiday—"

"And me heading to London to meet Haley's parents, Gabe holding things down in the city, you're the best option," Jacques explains.

"But only if you feel up to it." Gabe searches my eyes, as if looking for confirmation that I can handle the task.

"West can come stay with you too," Jacques points out.

I smile at Jacques. "You're meeting her family? Are you nervous?"

"After the you announced your pregnancy with your ex-boyfriend the first time she came to the vineyard? I think I'll be fine," he says dryly.

I grin at my brothers. "You will be. And I'll be fine, too! Truly. You"—I point to Jacques—"have a great time in London. And you"—I gesture toward Gabe—"hold shit down."

They both snicker.

"I'll see if West wants to tag along but he's ramping up his workouts as training camp grows closer. I'm surprised he stayed this long," I mumble, almost as an afterthought. "I think he's heading back to Knoxville for a mandatory team meeting soon, too."

Gabe shrugs. "I'm sure he'll fly right back to Paris when it's over."

"Yeah," I murmur.

But West's impending departure is starting to take up space at the forefront of my mind.

How long will West remain in Paris? And then…what? What happens when he leaves for good? For training camp? How are we going to raise our baby living in two different countries? Should I move to Knoxville? Will I be giving up everything I worked for here? And why the hell doesn't West seem stressed out about the future the way I am?

"Nov?" Gabe clears his throat.

"Hmm?" I glance up.

"You okay?" Jacques ask, peering at me.

I wave a hand. "Yes. Just…thinking. You know? A few days at Dad's house will be good for me too. I could use the fresh air and the…simplicity of it."

Gabe looks skeptical, Jacques tilts his head, but I force a smile and beam back.

"Honestly, guys, I got this!" I promise.

West stares at me over the rim of his coffee mug. "You're going to your dad's. For a week," he repeats my words, making sense of them.

"My brothers don't want him on his own if Deb's on holiday and I agree with them. It's only a few days," I continue.

West nods, turning the mug in his hands. "No, I get it. You should be there." The left side of his mouth lifts in a half smile. "I just hate being away from you, but I'm sorry, Nov, I can't skip out on my trainer for a full week."

Ah, he wants to tag along but can't.

I'd be lying if I admitted that a small part of me isn't disappointed. After all, a tiny, little slice of my mind was already envisioning all the things I would show West at my childhood home. The tire swing on the tree that Jacques built me. The little pond where I used to feed the ducks. And then, the rows on rows of vines. The old cellar. Wine tasting and charcuterie board making.

But the fact that he's here, in France, is already huge. "I understand." I do, too. "The season is coming up and—"

"Shh." West leans forward to press a kiss to my lips. "Do we have to talk about that now?" he mumbles, tugging my body into his frame.

I go willingly, straddling him in my kitchen, my arms winding around his neck. "We have to talk about it some-time," I say softly.

West pulls back slightly to catch my eyes. "I know, Nov. I just… I hate that there's a countdown clock in both of our minds. Because no matter what happens, we're a family now. Me, you, and our little. And I won't let either of you go."

I nod, even as tears flood my eyes, turning my vision blurry. "Is that a promise?"

"Take it to the bank," he murmurs.

"What?" I sputter, shaking my head. "I've never heard that expression."

West laughs. "It's actually something my dad used to say." He shakes his head. "It's weird. I've gone the last fifteen years hardly giving him a thought. And now…"

I thread my fingers through the hair on the nape of his neck. "Do you think of him often now?"

West shrugs, avoiding my gaze before sighing. Then, he looks at me. "All these thoughts from my childhood. Things I forgot about, suddenly, they're there. It's like I'm reliving them. Remembering shit I'd rather forget." He shakes his head. "Weird, right?"

"I think having a baby brings up a lot of emotions. It's normal to be reminded of your own childhood when you're considering what your kid's childhood is going to look like," I say slowly. "I've been thinking about my mom more, too."

His brows pull together. "You have?"

"Yeah. I miss her. She was…she was wonderful, West. She used to sing me to sleep and do all the characters' voices when she read me books. We'd bake on Sunday mornings, and she always kept the cookie jar full."

West smiles. "When you talk about your childhood, it makes me feel hopeful for our kid's. I didn't have anything like that, Nova. But, fuck, it makes me happy that you did."

I inch myself closer to him, pressing my fingertips into the heat of his skin. "Do you want to talk about it?"

He snorts, glancing down at the hardening bulge in his pants. "Not at this exact moment."

I laugh. But my tone is serious as I ask, "But one day? Soon?"

West's hands frame my hips, then slide around to my ass. His large palms settle, and he squeezes. "Soon," he promises, lowering his mouth to mine.

I tip my head back as he slides my body forward until my

core connects with his erection and his mouth slams over mine. Then, West stands and carries me to the bedroom, where he makes me forget our conversation, our long-distance dilemma, and even my own name.

Instead, I call out his.

17

WEST

"She's at her dad's house. I have about five days to pull everything together," I confide in Allegra.

"Eek! I am beyond exited for this," Allegra gushes through FaceTime. "I spoke to my interior designer Taylor, and she put together a few mood boards. I'm emailing them now. Let me know what you think of the color palettes, and we can move forward from there."

"Thanks, A," I mutter, pulling up my inbox on my laptop.

"How'd you get Nova to spend time at her Dad's?"

"Her brothers came up with the idea. Then they enlisted Claude's help. Something about him not being able to stay on his own while their housekeeper is out of town," I explain.

"Seriously?" Allegra snorts. "That's cold-blooded. They've got Nova thinking her dad is having another health scare?"

I shake my head. "I don't think they worded it like that."

"Implied," Allegra counters.

I snort. "Maybe. It actually does put everyone's minds at ease but, for my purposes, it worked like a charm."

"Yeah," Allegra agrees.

"Okay, I'm looking at the mood boards," I mutter. "Shit, I never thought I'd say those words aloud."

"Get used to it!"

I chuckle. "I like the one with green and…wood."

"The thyme and batton board." Allegra nods. "I like that one too."

"Claude mentioned—"

"Oh! First name basis with Nova's dad. I see you, Crawford."

I snort. "That he has the bassinet from when Nova was a baby. He'd like to give it to us, and I said yes."

"Really?" Excitement flares in Allegra's eyes. "Can you send me a photo?"

"Um, sure." I snap a picture of the basket Jacques delivered and send it to her.

"Aww," she coos. "It's a proper Moses basket."

"Okay." What the hell? I don't know half the things Allegra is talking about. How do women just…know these things?

"And there's a stand. That's perfect for the early days."

"Great," I say, sounding relieved that it's one less thing to think about.

"Taylor's going to love this!"

"Thanks for helping with this, Allegra. I can definitely do this wall. And I want to build bookshelves on the other side, near the rocking chair."

Allegra's expression softens as she smiles at me.

"What?" I ask.

"You're doing great, West. This"—she makes a circle on the screen with her hand—"is a look I like. I'm happy for you."

A strange sense of pride rises in my chest, and I clear my throat to shake off the embarrassment. "Uh, thanks."

"Okay," she sighs, snapping out of it. "I'll get a list of paint colors over to you. Taylor will draw out where you should paint what based on the photos of the room you provided. Also, I'll send links to everything you need to order."

"I already ordered that little lamb rocker."

"You did?" She squeals. "Okay, should we coordinate the delivery options?"

I laugh. "I'm just going to give you my credit card, A."

"That's what Derek suggested too."

"Smart man."

"Let's discuss the party." She changes gears.

"You really think we can pull this off?"

"A baby shower? Totally!" Allegra waves a hand.

"But she's not due until November—"

"You'll be in season then."

"I don't want to freak her out or—"

"She's going to love it!"

"Will people think we're being hasty and—"

"Since when do you care what people think?" Allegra lifts both eyebrows.

I sigh.

"Wesley," she scolds.

"You know that's not my name, right?"

She shrugs. "It sounds more appropriate for chiding."

I snort. "My full name is West."

"Seriously?"

"Seriously. And I don't care except... Allegra, I'm becoming a dad."

She smiles. "I know."

"I just wanna do the right thing. Do right by my kid."

"Trust me, Wesley, creating the perfect nursery and hosting a baby shower for Nova are both beautiful, thoughtful things. Don't overthink what you feel is right for you and your family."

I nod slowly, letting my mind absorb her words. I'm not used to questioning myself like this. But with Nova, with our baby, I don't want to misstep. I want to be the kind of man they both can rely on. I want to be the opposite of my father. "You're right."

"I know."

"Thanks, A."

"Anytime. Mckenna and Ivy already booked their flights. Jameson can't make it, but Mav, Levi, and Derek are in. We arrive next Thursday and will have everything sorted for Saturday morning."

"I've booked the venue."

"You're seriously hosting a baby shower at The George-Louis Hotel?"

I laugh. "Yep. Go big or go home, right?"

"Right."

"And I'm not going home without Nova."

Allegra sucks in a breath. "West, you have training camp and—"

"We'll figure it out before then," I say, my mind made up.

Allegra's right. Why the hell am I second-guessing myself? Since when do I give a shit what others think of me? My priority is Nova and our baby. My family.

And I will create a perfect nursery. I will throw my girl the most exquisite baby shower. And it doesn't matter where our home base is—Knoxville or Paris—I'm not leaving without knowing that Nova and I are building a future together.

Nova: (image of tire swing)

Nova: This is the tire swing Jacques built me as a kid.

Me: I can build a tire swing.

Nova: (laughing face emoji) I know you can.

Me: We can get a big chunk of land outside of Knoxville...

Me: Our little can run around outside all the time.

Nova: And swing on a tire swing?

Me: Yup.

Being apart from Nova for the last few days is tough. I miss her. I miss checking to see if her belly filled out a little more. I want to note all the physical changes in her body, watch the wonder in her eyes grow, and be a part of this journey. Every single step.

But I wrapped up the baby's nursery this morning. As I stand in the bedroom door and look at the space, I'm proud of what I created. It's soft and sweet and the perfect place to bring a baby home. We still don't know if Nova will be in Knoxville or Paris in November. But it doesn't matter. Our baby will always have a home in Knoxville and a space in Paris—and will need rooms to claim in both.

I pull up the photo on my phone that Allegra's designer Taylor sent. Then, I get to work setting up the decor. When I'm done, I've transformed the room into a proper nursery. My fingers graze over the little lamb rocker.

Vaguely, I remember having one like this—except, it was a horse—as a kid. My dad broke it in a moment of rage but there were moments when I rocked as fast as I could, whooped like a cowboy, and laughed until tears trickled down my cheeks.

For all the horrible memories, I like when a positive one pops up.

I take a photo of the room and text it to Allegra. I'm slipping my phone back in my pocket when it rings.

"Hey, Cal," I answer.

"West. How's the do-it-yourself project going?"

"Actually, I just finished it."

"And?"

"Not gonna lie, Callie, I'm pretty proud of how it turned out," I admit, my tone softer than it was a second ago. Jesus, is Nova's emotional state transferring to me?

I send Callie the picture I just took.

I know when she receives it because she gasps. I grin.

"West!" Callie—calm, collected, celebrated sports agent—squeals. "This is gorgeous. Wow. You did all of it?"

"Have a little faith."

"It's only because it looks so…professional."

"I had some help," I admit. "A designer Allegra is friends with—"

"Yeah, with the decor. But you did that accent wall? The bookshelves?"

I look at the batten wall. "I did."

"Well done, Crawford. Seriously."

"Thanks, Cal. Are you coming for the baby shower?"

She laughs, like she can't believe this is happening. "I'll be there," she confirms.

"Good. I want you to meet Nova. You'll love her."

"I'm sure."

"I take it you're not calling just about my nursery progress?" I ask, switching gears.

Callie sighs and my stomach sinks. "I'm not. I spoke with Claudette."

"And?"

"There are terms," she says slowly.

I drag my hand over my hair. "I'm not going to like them, am I?"

"Not even a little," Callie confirms.

I close the nursery door and relocate to the living room. Sitting on the sofa, I don't lean back since it's like resting on marble. Instead, I heave out a sigh. "Lay it on me."

"Marisa wants to be the one to initiate the breakup," Callie starts.

"Done."

"Green Moose Athletics still wants the two of you to represent the brand. And to do the photoshoot together."

Shit. I scratch my cheek. "Nothing we can do about that. I mean, the optics won't be great but—"

"Marisa will back out. She'll let you take the account without her involvement."

I work a swallow, nerves gathering in my stomach. "But?"

"She wants you at the Milan show. She wants you to sit in the front row, support her, and shout it out on your socials. You've garnered quite the following from your season and, even though you've been quiet, your posts will help generate more press coverage for the event. Then, she'll break up with you and decline the offer from Green Moose."

"Ahh," I groan, tipping my head back. "I don't want to go to a fucking fashion show. For Marisa."

"I know."

"But I want Green Moose. Solo, without having to work with her. And, if the campaign is successful, I don't want to continue working with her."

"Yeah," Callie agrees. "Can I make a suggestion?"

"Have at it."

"Why don't you discuss this with Nova? See what she thinks. Include her in the decision-making process. And let me know what you decide."

I blow out an exhale. Loop Nova in. Callie's right. I need to give Nova a heads-up, so she doesn't think I'm going behind her back to see Marisa. Or whatever the fuck she'll think depending on how the media covers the event. "That's a good idea, Cal."

"I'm known for them, West."

"I'll talk to Nova about it. But the baby shower is next week…"

"And the fashion show is right after. Timing and optics could be tricky, but the baby shower is a small, intimate gathering. We'll have extra security and…it's a good thing you're in Paris. People aren't as interested in your life there."

"True," I laugh. "Which has been nice."

"I bet. Don't forget, a few days after Milan, you need to be in Knoxville for that team meeting."

I wince. How the hell did I forget about the mandatory team meeting the Coyotes called? I wonder why they need us to gather in person when an email would probably suffice. "Okay, I'll talk to Nova and get back to you," I decide.

"Sounds good. Speak soon, West." Callie ends the call.

I send the image of the nursery to my teammates and stand.

While the conversation with Callie could have been better, it also could have gone worse. In two weeks, I can be free of my fake relationship with Marisa Mella, have a great endorsement deal intact, and focus all my attention on Nova and our baby.

Or I could break the terms of my contract and let the endorsement deal go right now?

But will Marisa take to social media and cause more damage? Maybe imply that I cheated on her with Nova or shit like that?

While I don't think Marisa is vindictive, she is shrewd. She's smart. And she will use whatever resources she has to produce the best outcome for her career.

I pinch the bridge of my nose. The last thing I want to do is cause Nova stress. Or have a bunch of publications report shit that our little could dig up and read one day.

No, I have to be smart about this decision. I need to take the path that bests protects my family.

I need to talk to Nova.

18

Nova

"SHE WANTS YOU TO GO TO MILAN?" I INQUIRE, MAKING SURE I'm hearing West correctly.

"Yeah," he sighs, frustrated. "She'll step away from the Green Moose contract—"

"Which you really want."

"I do," he admits. "But I'm more worried about the optics of you being pregnant and me being in a fake relationship with Marisa at the same time."

"They'd paint me a homewrecker," I murmur.

"Or me a two-timing son of a bitch," he replies.

"What does Marisa think?" Everything West has told me about Marisa Mella is that she is a professional, intelligent businesswoman, focused on her career.

"She wants to get as much press on this fashion show as possible. I think the designer, Hansen Cross, is a friend. And she's hoping to become the face of more luxury brands. Haute couture instead of streetwear or athletic brands like Green Moose."

"And you provide that?" I wonder.

"Our *relationship* provides that. It's an added level of interest from the public," he clarifies, his voice tight. "Fuck, it's stupid. I'll call it off. Just admit it was a fake relationship that—"

"No," I interject, thinking things through. "Don't be hasty. We're…communicating. Talking this out. That's good. You worked really hard to get where you are, West. We can figure this out without you blowing up the image you're trying to create." I pause, turning things over in my mind. "I think you should go."

He swears softly.

"I don't want you to miss out on this endorsement deal because of one appearance that could have nipped everything in the bud," I continue. "Isn't that why you started your fake PR stunt in the first place? To try to get endorsement deals?"

"Yeah," he mutters.

"And you'll be cultivating the family man reputation once we share that we're back together and pregnant. There's definitely a way to positively spin our story as long as Marisa is on our side and doesn't take to social media portraying a different view. That's why it's imperative that she break up— or whatever—with you. And you just show up at a fashion show and pose for some photos. It's not the end of the world." As much as I hate the fact that he'll have to go and play along with this stupid lie at her side, it really is the simplest way out of the predicament. The option that causes the least harm. The one that…nips shit in the bud.

West is silent for a long time. Then, "Are you sure you're okay with this? Because I fucking hate that I'm putting you in this position at all."

"You made this deal before we were back together," I remind him. "And you partly made it because we weren't together."

"I never want to hurt you, Nova." The sincerity in his voice sweeps through me.

"I know. It's just…a fashion show and some posed photos, right?"

"Right," he agrees quickly. Then, he sighs heavily. "But, a few days after the show, I need to head to Knoxville for a mandatory team meeting."

"I know. You told me," I say softly.

"I just hate being away from you."

"Me too, West," I agree. "But we'll figure it out. One thing at a time. Call Callie and tell her you're in. Then, in a few weeks, we can start crafting how to share our news with the world."

"I can't wait," West admits, a smile in his tone. "I miss you."

"I miss you, too. I'll be home in three days."

"Okay."

"Call Callie," I remind him sternly.

"I will," he promises. "I'm just heading to the gym first."

"Have a good workout."

West snorts. "'Bye, baby."

"Bye," I say, ending our call.

"All good?" Dad asks.

I jump, my hand flying to my chest. "You scared me!"

"Sorry." He doesn't sound sorry at all.

"No, you're not."

Dad laughs.

"You were eavesdropping." I point at him.

He pours me a mug of tea and places it in front of me. "It's hardly eavesdropping if you're talking in the kitchen." He gestures around the open living space. "This is communal."

I roll my eyes. "West needs to go to a fashion show with his fake girlfriend to get out of the contract with the least amount of blowback."

Dad lifts an eyebrow.

I explain about the Green Moose endorsement and Marisa's insistence that West show up to the fashion show before they part ways.

Dad nods and takes a sip of his tea, leaning against the kitchen countertop. "And you're okay with this?"

I shrug. "It sucks. I mean, I'm not happy about it. But I do think it's the best way forward—one event and done—and after next week, we move on from it."

"True," Dad agrees. "You're not showing yet either, which is helpful."

I laugh. "I may not be showing but all my pants are starting to feel…snug."

"Gabe will take you shopping if you ask."

I arch an eyebrow. "Yeah, he took West shopping."

"I noticed." Dad smiles. "Loafers."

We both laugh.

"I missed this more than I realized." I look around the kitchen. "Being home, hanging out."

"Me too." Dad's eyes lighten. "I'm happy you're home, Nova. Even if you decide not to stay."

I pull in a sharp breath.

"Don't tell me you haven't thought about it," Dad says.

"Of course, I have," I admit. But am I ready to give up on everything I'm creating here? To take a leap of faith that big when the last time…it didn't work out. "But you've all given me leeway with the tasting room. Gabe and Jacques have entrusted me with accounts that they used to hold." I shake my head. "I can't just…leave."

"Your life changed in a big way, Nova. Just like mine did when I had that heart attack," Dad says slowly. "You stepped up for me. Came home, helped out, did everything everyone asked of you. Of course, we want you to stay. And yes, you are an asset to our family business. But this isn't a normal business; you're also my daughter. You're about to become a mom. You need to do what's in the best interest of *your* family, and that will always be what's best for *our* entire family." Dad grins and the familiar lines around his eyes crinkle. "Make the decision that's right for you and West and your baby. Don't worry about us. There will always be a place for you here in our home and at the company. But Gabe and Jacques are more than capable of taking back those accounts. We can hire extra staff. We have resources to tap into, whatever you decide."

My dad's thoughtfulness hits me in my feels. As usual, I nearly cry. God, I can't wait until this part of the pregnancy journey is behind me. Feeling weepy makes me cringe. I swallow back the emotions and give my dad a smile. "Thank you, Daddy. I love you."

He rounds the kitchen island to embrace me. Dropping a kiss to the top of my head, he murmurs, "You'll always be my baby, Nov. Trust me, as a parent, the thing you want most is to see your kids happy. I love you, too."

We spend the rest of the day hanging out, watching movies, and talking. At one point, Dad pulls out some photo albums from my childhood and we pour over them, reminiscing and laughing. Spending this week with him makes me realize how special our relationship is. It fills me with excitement for the bond I'll cultivate with my child. And it also infuses me with hope to witness the type of father West will grow into.

"What are we doing here?" I ask Jacques as he leads me into The George-Louis Hotel.

"I just have to drop off an envelope," he explains.

"For what?" I shake my head, bewildered. "Are you sure Haley is okay too? She left Dad's house pretty quickly. And since when do you trust a girlfriend with your car?"

Jacques snorts. "Haley's fine. It's a work thing and she takes her career very seriously."

I roll my eyes.

"Plus, she's a fantastic driver. Came up in the karting circuits with her brothers."

"Seriously?" My eyes widen. "That's...badass."

"Right?" Jacques agrees. "It's just through here." He leads me down a hallway and points toward one of the event spaces. "My client is at some conference."

"Okay." I follow after him.

Jacques pulls open the large door and tips his head. "After you."

Surprise crosses my face. I don't want to walk into the middle of a conference—what type of conference is it, anyway?

Jacques lifts his eyebrows, waiting.

I sigh and step through the door.

"Surprise!" The word rings out and I stumble back half a step.

Luckily, my brother is already behind me and places a steadying hand on my shoulder.

"Oh my God," I murmur, looking around the gorgeous space.

The room is boxed off to make it cozy and intimate. A large chandelier hangs from the ceiling. A fireplace blazes in the corner, giving off a soft glow. Everything is decorated in sage green, shades of cream, and white.

Comfortable chairs cluster around circular tables. Each table has a beautiful centerpiece of flowers and sweet stuffed animals. There's a long, harvest table with the largest charcuterie display I've ever seen. Greenery adds delicate details to the grazing table, along with flowers in various vases and a smattering of tea lights.

West comes forward, rubbing his hands together nervously. "Are you surprised?"

I beam. "You did this?"

"I had some help."

Allegra, Ivy, and Mckenna scurry closer, and my mouth falls open.

"What are you doing here?" I ask. My hand lifts to my mouth, covering it, as tears—always the tears!—slip onto my cheeks.

"As if we'd miss your baby shower," Ivy scoffs.

"Don't you dare cry!" Allegra warns.

"I'm so happy for you," Mckenna says, opening her arms.

I hug her and our other friends gather around, until we're in a little huddle.

"I had no idea. I can't believe this," I say.

"West did an awesome job," Mckenna agrees.

"This is some college girl huddle," Ivy laughs.

I pull away from my friends and laugh, wiping my tears away. I glance over Allegra's head to a patiently waiting West.

"Sorry!" I gush.

But he's grinning at me, like he's just happy to see me surprised.

I run my hands over my hips and glance down. "I would have worn—"

"Don't worry. I brought you options," Ivy says.

I sigh. "Thank God."

My friends laugh as I move toward my man. West draws me into his arms and kisses me sweetly.

"Thank you, West," I say. "This is the most incredible surprise."

"I love you, Nova. I love the life we're building."

His words are tender and sweet. Honest and thoughtful. "I love you, too."

He kisses me again before Gabe groans.

"Cut that shit out," my brother teases.

I laugh and give him a hug. "Thanks for coming."

"As if I'd miss this," Gabe says, pointing out Haley and our father over by the bar.

"This is where Haley disappeared to!" I gush.

Haley gives me a little wave and a big grin.

"Congratulations, Nov," Mav Tate says, wrapping me in a hug.

"Happy for you," Levi tacks on.

"Good to see you, Nova," Derek says, kissing my cheek.

"You guys!" I beam at The Burnt Clovers members. Opening my arms, I pull them all into a hug. "Thanks for being here."

"You're the first in our crew to get knocked up," Levi explains.

"Yep," Mav confirms. "We're doing it big for you since I'm sure the novelty will rub off."

Derek laughs as Allegra sticks her tongue out at him.

"Come on!" West says, pulling me deeper into the room. "I want you to meet my agent. And I'd like you to introduce me to some of your friends. Your brothers helped with the guest list. Plus, there's some dessert I don't know how to pronounce that—"

"West," I cut off his nervous rambling.

He gazes at me. "Yeah?"

"You're going to be the best daddy."

He smiles. "I hope so, Nova."

"I know so," I confirm.

"All right!" Allegra claps her hands together once West and I are in the center of the space, with our family and friends surrounding us. "Let's celebrate Baby Crawford."

As the realization settles in that our baby will have West's last name, emotions sweep his features. I stare at him, memorizing the light in his eyes, the hope in his smile, and the pure love he showers me with.

19

WEST

"One more gift," I say as I place down the last bag filled with presents. Nova's baby shower was a huge success and I loved spending the day watching my woman beam with happiness.

"More?" Nova shakes her head. "Impossible! There must be a hundred presents here!" She gestures toward the pile placed along the wall in her living room.

"Come here." I step closer to take her hand and tug her toward the baby's nursery.

"What is it?" She yawns.

I hide my smile. She has no idea, and I can't wait to surprise her. Again. Catching my supernova off guard is quickly becoming one of my favorite hobbies.

I stop outside the nursery door. Nova gazes up at me, her eyes wide. "What's wrong?"

"Nothing." I shake my head. "Open it."

Her eyes fill with moisture and her mouth twists, as if she already knows what's coming. Tenderness streaks her gaze as she blinks at me. "West."

"Open the door, Nov."

She nods and grips my hand tighter before using her free

hand to turn the knob, push the door open, and step inside. I reach above her head to flick on the light.

She inhales audibly. "Oh, it's so beautiful."

Her eyes widen as she raises a hand to her lips. Then, she looks at me. "You did this, too?"

"I did."

"The wall and the bookshelves?"

"I've got moves too, Martin."

Nova laughs—that musical symphony I fucking love— and turns into my frame. I wrap my arms around her waist as she clutches me close. "West, this is too much."

"I'm just getting started, baby."

She tips her head back and I note the love shimmering in her gaze. "Thank you. You made today—all of this—so special. Thank you."

"It is special, Nova. You're special, our baby is...already the best thing that's ever happened to me." I bend to kiss her hard.

When I pull back, she smiles. "I love this room. I love everything about it." She releases me to look around the space.

She stops to grin at the framed photo of us—the parents— on our little's dresser. "This was from Derek and Allegra's BBQ. The last photo we took together before..."

"Yeah." Before we broke up.

She picks up the frame. "You had this picture at your place in Knoxville."

"On my dresser." I squeeze the back of my neck, feeling uncomfortable. "I took it with me."

Nova looks at me. "To Paris?"

I shrug sheepishly. "To everywhere. I travel with it. To all my away games...wherever."

Her lips part and softness rolls over her face. "Really?"

"You're always with me, Nov," I admit. "And I want to always be with our little, even if I'm not here all the time."

She nods slowly, placing the frame down. She looks at the bookshelf next, checking out each little knickknack—a baby bank, more picture frames, a snow globe—as well as the collection of children's books in English and French. "I loved this book as a kid. My mom used to read it to me," she whispers, picking up the copy of *I'll Love You Forever* by Robert Munsch.

"Check out the rocker." I point to the little lamb.

Nova giggles, giving it a little shake. "This is the sweetest."

I clear my throat. "I had something like this as a kid. Except, it was a horse."

She eyes me curiously, as if waiting for me to continue.

I sigh. I don't want to ruin such a good day with the shit of my childhood but…I want to tell her things too.

"It's hard for me to imagine what our baby's life will look like. I never thought I'd have kids."

Surprise flashes in her eyes.

"Not that I didn't want them," I rush to explain, crossing the baby's room and sitting down in the rocking chair. I plant my feet on the floor and press back in the chair, half looking at the ceiling as I collect my thoughts.

I lift my feet and rush forward.

"Just that this would never be my life," I explain, gesturing around the room. "Why would any woman want to build a life with me? The son of a murderer."

Nova straightens, her lips pressing into a line as she waits for me to continue.

"My dad was tough. He beat my mom. He beat me. He was a drunk, narcissistic asshole. But my mom…she fucking loved him. Even though he put her in the hospital. Even though he laid his hands on me."

"West," Nova's voice breaks.

I shake my head. I need to get this out. "She always went back to him. Until she couldn't. He was charged with the murder of three teenagers, Nova. They were practically kids. And he killed them. He tortured them and played sick fucking head games with them for hours in the woods before putting bullets in their heads."

Nova swears, striding across the room.

I hold out my hand. My palms itch and my ears ring. But I need to tell her the rest. When we were dating, I gave her snippets, but never the full story. But now, we're having a baby. We're...moving forward. And I need to confide in her. I need to get it out and have her know the things I never speak of. Probably because they're fucking unspeakable. Unthinkable. Unconscionable.

"He's serving life in prison for his crimes," I continue. "But my mom, she couldn't take it. She slit her wrists in the bathtub a few weeks after his sentencing. I found her—"

"West," Nova's voice cracks as tears stream down her cheeks. I'd told her my mother killed herself but never how. Never the scene I witnessed when I opened the bathroom door.

"And I called 9-1-1. But it was too late. After that, I bounced around the foster care system, moving from one family to the next. I tried to protect the other kids in whatever house I was living in whenever shit went sideways."

She nods. I've told her some of my foster care experiences. I've talked more about that than my own parents.

I sigh. "That shit happened often. I did my best. And you know the rest."

"You went all in on football," she murmurs.

"When Coach Kent gave me a shot, I took it." I manage a smile. "See? Someone gave me a chance."

"I'm sorry he's not here to see the man you grew into." Nova drops to her knees in front of me. She places her hands on my legs and stares up at me with wide, tearful eyes and heartache in the lines of her face.

"Don't kneel before me," I growl out. I don't want her on

the fucking ground. Instead, I pull her up, situate her on my lap, and cradle her against my chest.

"He was a good man. The best I've ever known," I admit. My high school football coach believed in me in a way that no one else ever has. Until Nova. He died in a car accident my freshman year of college, and in some ways, his death affected me even deeper than my parents' betrayal.

"He was your role model," Nova whispers.

"Yeah," I agree. "He was. Still is."

She turns in my arms and gives me a soft smile. "Thank you for telling me everything. I knew bits and pieces but…"

"It's a lot."

"It's your story," she replies.

"I never want our baby to have a story like that. I'm not even a dad yet and I already know that I'd never fucking want any of that shit to touch my kid."

"It won't," she swears.

Her words from weeks ago come back to me.

You didn't get a fair shot but that doesn't mean you don't know how to give one.

"You mean everything to me, Nova. You and our baby. And I am fucking terrified of losing you again." My voice cracks at the thought. I already know I couldn't bear it.

Nova cups my cheek and I lean into her touch.

"You won't, West. We're a family now. We've got this." She takes my hand and places it on the softest little swell of her belly. No one could tell Nova is pregnant from looking at her, but I note the subtle changes. The little shifts. The sweet swell.

I brush my fingers below her belly button and splay my hand wide.

"I can't wait to meet him or her," I admit.

"Me neither," she says. "West, I know we said we'd wait for the baby's birth but…do you want to find out the sex of the baby?"

Our twenty-week scan is in nine days.

I roll my lips together. "I really can't wait but…I'm down for the surprise. Nova, how many good surprises like this do we really get?"

"Well, after today…" She pauses and bites her bottom lip shyly. "I'm really enjoying the good surprises too."

"Then we'll wait and be surprised," I agree.

Nova stares at me for a long beat before leaning forward. She kisses me softly. Her lips glide over mine, light and sweet. "Thank you for today, West."

"Thank you for every day, Nov," I reply, threading my fingers through her hair. I angle her head as she deepens our kiss, slipping her tongue into my mouth. She begins to shift in my arms but right now, I want her in our bedroom, where I can undress her slowly, marvel at her beautiful body, and take her without the little lamb rocker staring at me.

I gather Nova in my arms and stand, carrying her from our baby's nursery to the bedroom. She winds her arms around my neck as I lay her in the center of the bed. I shift over her, peeling the winter white dress Ivy brought over her shoulders, down her torso, and past her hips until I toss it on the floor.

"You're so beautiful." I graze my hand from her chin, between the valley of her breasts, over the soft swell I'm now obsessed with, and to the waistband of her lace panties. I drag my fingers over the lace, loving that her breath hitches. God, she makes me fucking crazy in the best way possible.

Dropping one knee to the bed, I hover over Nova. I cage her in between my arms and as I dip my head, she lifts her face to meet my kiss. Our lips fuse and our kiss turns passion-ate. Nova arches into me as I press down on her. Our hands touch as our mouths take. Nova's love dulls the hurt of my childhood. Her compassion eases the complicated feelings of abandonment and fear I carry around. Instead, her love is healing. And God, do I want to be healed. Whole. Loved.

"Nova," I whisper.

"I'm right here," she says, pulling my sweater over my head and discarding it. Her fingers unbutton my pants next, and I work them over my hips.

"I need you."

"You have me," she promises.

"I need…" I trail off.

"Show me, West." Nova takes my hand and places it on the center of her chest. Her fingers wrap around my wrist, anchoring me to her. "Show me."

So, I do.

I make love to her. I show her—through my actions, my words, and the way I fulfill every single one of her needs—how much she means to me.

She means every fucking thing.

I show her how much she affects me.

She turns my world upside down.

And I revel in the depth of my love for her.

Endless and infinite.

IT'S WITH WEST'S KISS ON MY LIPS AND HIS SCENT LINGERING ON my pillow that he leaves for the airport.

"I'll be back tomorrow night," he assures me.

"I know." But my body feels cloaked in insecurity. Uncertainty. Doubt. Ugh, I hate that. I know this is West's work. It's an appearance so he can secure a greater opportunity.

It's business.

But I still feel like throwing up at the thought of West cheering on a beautiful and glamorous Marisa Mella in Milan while I sit here and fret. Feeling frumpy as fuck now that my jeans don't button.

"Nov." West's voice is tight. "Tell me what you're thinking. I can see the wheels turning, babe."

I huff. Toss a hand in the air. Narrow my eyes at him. "I'm…frustrated."

He smiles which only heightens my annoyance.

"Come here." He wraps an arm around me. "I thought you were going to finish the tasting room while I'm gone? Surprise me when I get back?"

"My jeans don't fit," I lament instead, focused on the important things in my life.

West holds me closer, and I feel his suppressed chuckle

rattle in his chest. "Then don't wear 'em." He grabs a handful of my ass and gives it a squeeze. "I prefer you pantless anyway."

I pull back and give him a look, rolling my eyes. "Yeah, you and every other guy that—"

His eyes darken and he cuts me off. "Don't finish that sentence, Nov."

I harrumph for good measure.

West's eyes soften. He bends down to kiss me hard. "Finish your tasting room. Wear sweatpants. And when I'm back, we'll go shopping and I'll follow you around from store to store and hold all the bags."

I snort, even though the picture he's painting is appealing. West hates shopping in stores and prefers to order everything online or have someone shop for him. I'm still shocked Gabe managed to drag him out. "Fine."

"Good." He kisses me again. "Anything else before I go?"

"No. I'll probably sleep at my dad's tonight," I add as an afterthought.

West nods. "I think you should. I hate the thought of you being alone overnight."

I tilt my head. "What do you think is going to happen when you're in Knoxville and I'm—"

His neck swivels and he glares at me. I sigh.

I'm trying to pick a fight because I'm annoyed, and we both know it.

"I'll see you tomorrow," I say, because I'm not apologizing for shit.

West nods. "Tomorrow, baby."

Then, he grasps the handle of his suitcase and moves toward the front door. I watch him leave, knowing that the car is already idling by the curb to whisk him to the airport.

The second West is gone, the space feels emptier. "Argh!" I stomp around, my frustration mounting.

Swiping my phone, I message the girls.

Me: West is en route to Milan.

Ivy: Yikes! How are you taking it?

I roll my eyes. My friends know that sometimes, I've got a short fuse. Just because I logically understand the merits of something doesn't mean I can check my emotions on it. I slam the refrigerator door closed after grabbing a carton of milk.

Case in point.

Me: FINE.

Ivy: LIAR.

Me: I'm annoyed.

Ivy: I would be too.

Mckenna: You know it's only for a fashion show. Throw yourself into work and West will be back before you know it.

Allegra: Are you actually worried about things or just…pissed off?

Me: Pissed off.

Ivy: Do something fun today. Screw work. Enjoy your life.

Me: Ha!

Me: Not a bad idea.

Me: IDK what the fuck to do with myself.

Mckenna: Finish your tasting room so it's done, and you can enjoy more time with West when he's back.

Allegra: So practical.

Mckenna: (smirking face emoji) I prefer results driven.

Me: My brother is calling... BRB

"Hello?" I answer the phone.

"Sulking?" Gabe asks, knowing me well.

"West called you, didn't he?"

"As soon as he pulled away from the curb," Gabe confirms.

"I'm fine."

He chortles. "I'm picking you up for brunch."

"Really?" I ask, feeling my annoyance fade. A teeny tiny bit. My brother's thoughtfulness envelops me, and I manage a smile. "At La tassa à thé?"

Gabe laughs. "Yes. To the teacup, you pain in the ass."

"Okay! I'm getting dressed."

"See you in twenty." He hangs up.

Mckenna: Plans?

Me: Gabe is taking me to brunch.

Ivy: You really are the baby of the family.

Me: Jealous?

Ivy: You have no idea.

Ivy is the eldest of four and I've witnessed how her responsibilities and obligations outweigh mine by lightyears. In fact, she probably has more in common with Jacques as far as family dynamics go.

Allegra: Go get ready. Have fun today! Don't worry about West. This whole thing will be over before you know it.

Me: Yeah, yeah. Love you, girls.

Ivy: Love you.

Mckenna: (red heart emoji)

I leave my phone on the coffee table as I hurry to get dressed for brunch. I opt for a powder blue, knee-length, slip skirt and an oversized, chunky white sweater. I pull on some heeled booties, shrug into my favorite cream-colored coat, and swap out my purse, dropping my phone in just as it buzzes.

I pull it out. "I'm ready!" I answer.

"Oh, um, hello? Nova?" a man's voice—news alert, it's not Gabe—comes through the line.

I frown and squint at the screen. Fuck. "Hi, Pierre! I'm sorry about that; I thought you were Gabe," I backtrack.

He chuckles. "No problem. How are you? Is this a bad time?"

I wince, hating the I'm going to blow him off when we really need to talk. While things between us have been fine since West punched him in the face—and he hasn't taken back the contracts to sell Martin Wine at two of his restaurants—there is a noticeable shift in our relationship. One I need to rectify because—business.

And yes, I realize how hypocritical I'm being. But I don't really care, either.

I soften my voice. "I'm just going to brunch with my brother. But I'm glad you called. We need to talk and—"

"I wanted to fill you in on the sales your family's wine has been doing in the restaurants," he interjects. But I hear the hopeful note in his tone. I shift uncomfortably, knowing I have to shut that down.

Even though I'm not romantically interested in Pierre, he is a good guy, and I don't relish the awkward conversation we need to have.

"That would be great," I say after a pause. "We should

chat numbers. Would you like to meet at the tasting room at —" I pause to glance at my watch.

"How about we have dinner?" he cuts in smoothly.

Internally, I groan. "I'm actually going to my father's this afternoon."

"A coffee, then?"

I close my eyes but relent. "Sure. Want to meet at the cafe next to the tasting room?"

"*Oui*," Pierre agrees. "I will see you there at 3 p.m.?"

"See you then."

"*Adieu, ma belle.*" He disconnects.

I drop the phone in my purse. "Shit."

It rings loudly and I jump.

"I'm coming!" I answer.

"You don't have to yell about it," Gabe replies.

I hang up on him and shoulder my purse. Stalking to the door, I let myself out of my flat and pause. I need to get myself together.

I'm going to hang out with my brother, do some work on the tasting room, meet Pierre for a casual business coffee where I will explain that I am in a relationship with West and having a baby (!!!), and then, I'll head to my dad's house for a delicious dinner and relax.

I straighten my shoulders and suck in a calming breath.

Good plan, Nova. You got this.

After giving myself a little pep talk, I carry on to Gabe's waiting car.

He gives me a look as I slide into the passenger seat. "You okay?"

I smile and he rears back at how unnatural it is. "I'm great!"

"You're such a fucking liar," he laughs as he pulls away from the curb.

I roll my eyes because…I'm trying to be an adult, okay? "Just, take me to brunch."

"I pray you have a daughter as demanding as you, Nova." Gabe makes a U-turn. "You have no idea what you're in for."

I smirk. "I'd love to have a daughter like me."

"Yeah?" He laughs. "Why?"

"I'm wonderful," I announce.

Gabe laughs heartily. "It's good that you think so."

I stick my tongue out at him. "West thinks so too." And on that retort, I settle down some.

West and I are fine. This fashion show isn't a big deal. We're good. Great even.

This will all be over before I know it.

21

WEST

"West! I'm so happy you could make it!" Marisa Mella bounds from the chair where she is having her makeup removed after the fashion show to rush me. Her arms are open, genuine joy washing over her expression, and I feel like I got kicked in the stomach.

Fuck.

I keep my arms at my sides, patting her elbow awkwardly as she hugs me. When she pulls back, she gives me a look and I force a smile.

"You were great. Very…fashiony," I bite out.

Marisa snorts. "Thanks for coming."

"West, how are you?" Claudette appears, pulling me from Marisa and over to the side of the room.

People mill about—hair stylists, makeup artists, wardrobe designers, and assistants. So many damn assistants. They all have headsets. And look panicked. Why? The show is over and, as far as I could tell, there were no serious mishaps.

"West." Claudette fixes me with a stern look once we're tucked behind a…floral wall?

I lift my eyebrows, waiting for her to continue.

She sighs. "Listen, I understand your priorities have changed since you and Marisa first entered into a contract."

I open my mouth to explain but she lifts her hand, halting me.

"But Marisa is still very much focused on her career and the goals she set out at the start of the year. She's happy for you that you've reconnected with your college girlfriend, but she needs you to play your part for the next twenty-four hours to ensure that this event, and her role in it, receives the positive attention she's after. Next week, she'll officially put out a statement that ends the arrangement between the two of you." Claudette brushes her hands together, as if it's that easy.

My throat tightens and my hands clench. "The show is over. What do we need to do? Take a few photos?"

Claudette shrugs. "Take Marisa out to dinner. Smile for the cameras."

"What cameras?"

Claudette laughs. "Trust me, the cameras will find you."

I pinch the bridge of my nose. "Okay. Fine. Dinner. And then, I'm going back to my hotel—"

"Your hotel has changed," she responds.

"What?"

"I moved your stay to the same hotel as Marisa. You have a room on her floor. Hm?" She lifts her eyebrow.

I feel nauseous. Fuck. Marisa wants everyone to truly think we're together. Which, fine, I understand her reasoning. But it puts me in a terrible position. A position I don't want to fucking be in.

"Your dinner reservation is in forty minutes. Marisa will have her hair taken down and her makeup removed. Then, she'll dress, and you can go," Claudette continues, her tone crisp. Professional.

Just like Marisa, this is all part of a larger picture. It's not personal. Hell, it doesn't mean anything. This…is a job.

I blink slowly. My mindset shifts as I accept that I came here to do a job. I signed a contract. I need to deliver.

And then, this will be behind me. I'll move forward with Nova. I can focus on our baby without the hint of a scandal following my family around.

"I need to make a phone call," I say, trying to bite back my anger.

"There's a conference room through that hallway that you can use for privacy." Claudette points to the door.

"Thanks." I'm already striding toward the door. The second I'm in the conference room, with the door closed, I call Callie.

"You okay?" she answers.

"What the fuck?" I seethe.

Callie sighs. "They made it into more, didn't they?"

"Did you know?" I demand.

"No," she says, honesty in her tone. "But I figured they'd try. It's…it's what I would do."

"Fuck. We're going for…dinner. Like on a fucking date."

Callie sighs. "I figured they'd rope you into dinner but… anything else?"

"They moved my hotel reservation."

"They what?" She sounds indignant.

"A room on her floor," I grind out.

"West, I had no idea. I'll call Claudette now and—"

"No," I cut her off, closing my eyes. "What's the point? If I don't give in and make this the damn production they want, they'll continue to hang shit over my head, right? At least, Marisa *could*. She could make things harder for me going forward. But, if I give her what she wants now…then, this will all be over. We'll 'break up' and I won't have this shit following me around."

Callie's quiet for a long moment. Thinking, no doubt. Then, "What do you want to do? I'll call off the whole thing if that's what you want."

"Do you think I'm right?" I ask.

"About Marisa holding things over your head? Maybe.

She's a successful woman. Extremely driven and professional. You're the one who is changing the terms of the contract and she's compromising with you, right?"

"Yeah," I bite out.

"So, if you renege now…"

"She'll be in the right to make things harder for me down the line."

"Possibly," Callie admits.

"The show's over. I'm already here. Dammit," I sigh. "Let's leave it as is. It's twenty-four hours. I'll give Nova a heads-up. And let me just get this shit over with."

"Okay. Keep me posted."

"I will." I hang up.

Then, I call Nova.

Instead of her sunny voice, I get her damn voicemail.

I end the call and send her a text.

> Me: Hey! Call me when you get a chance. I need to run something by you.

Glancing at my watch, I sigh. Then, I pull myself together and exit the conference room.

When I step into the main area again, I lock eyes with Marisa.

She gives me a knowing look and dips her chin.

It's fucking showtime.

"Smile," she says as she picks up her wine glass.

I force a grin and lift my glass. Then, I lean back in my chair.

This is the most pretentious fucking restaurant I've been in, and I've spent the last two months in Paris.

Marisa shakes her head. "I had no idea, West. Honestly. I thought you were reconnecting with an ex, and I thought, good for you. But a baby?" Her eyes soften. "How far along is Nova?"

"Second trimester," I reply. "Due November 3."

A real smile touches her mouth. "Congratulations, West. I'm really happy for you. Your partying days in Vegas didn't seem like the real you."

"No," I agree. "They weren't."

"Nova's from Paris?"

"She's American and French. Her family lives in France now. We dated in college, and she planned to move to Knoxville with me. Her father fell ill at the start of the season. She came home to help out and…we grew apart."

"But now, you're back together."

"Yes." I smile thinking about Nova. Talking about her helps me relax. Now that I've told Marisa the truth, our interaction has become friendlier. "I'm going to ask her to move to Knoxville with me."

"I'm sure she'll say yes," Marisa says, waving a hand.

I laugh. "I don't know. She's very determined to have her own life, her own career, independent of mine."

"Smart woman."

"The smartest," I agree. "But I don't want to miss a second of our little's life and if she's in Paris…"

"You'll miss more than seconds."

"Exactly."

"What does Nova do for work?"

"She's always wanted to be a fashion designer," I admit.

Marisa grins, her eyes brightening. "It's a wonderful, but competitive, field."

"So, I'm learning. But right now, Nova is working for her family business. They own a vineyard. Martin Wines."

Marisa's eyes flash. "Seriously? I love their wine!"

Of course, she does. "We'll send you some."

She tips her glass toward me. "I'm holding you to that."

"What about you? Are you…" I let the sentence trail off since I don't want to put her on the spot. But things between us have shifted and now, we're chatting like buddies. She hasn't acted romantic toward me at all.

"No." She shakes her head. "There's no time for anything meaningful."

"You have to make it a priority," I point out.

"Yes." She nods. "But I'm not willing to. Not right now. I was actually worried when you went to Paris about how that would look for us."

I snort. "No one there recognizes me. Or cares."

"A blessing," she agrees. "But now, I can't imagine how you'd stay away."

"I couldn't."

She gestures with her wine glass. "It's good this is our last appearance. I'll make a statement next week that we broke up weeks ago, after the gala in Washington DC. I'll say that you just came to the show to support me because we maintained a great friendship."

Surprise rocks through me. "Seriously?"

"Yeah," she laughs. "I know I'm all business, West. But I have a heart."

"Damn, that would be great, Marisa. Thanks."

She nods and lifts her glass in my direction. "To our last appearance."

I snort and clink glasses with her. "Good job today. The show was…good."

"You're so full of shit, West," she laughs. "It looked like someone was pulling splinters out of your toes while you were sitting in the front row."

I snort. "It wasn't my thing," I agree. I'd never been to a fashion show before. And, unless it's Nova's future fashion line, I have no desire to do so again.

Marisa takes a long pull of her wine, her eyes holding

mine over the rim. In them, I note the determination and dedication. I've witnessed it on the faces of opponents on the football field.

Apparently, the fashion industry isn't that different.

Marisa polishes off her wine. "Shall we get the check?"

I let out a sigh of relief and gesture to the waiter that I'll take the bill. I can't wait to get back to the hotel and call Nova again.

I pay for our dinner and do the gentlemanly thing of helping Marisa into her coat. When we're bundled up, we step onto the street.

"Ah, it's beautiful out. Want to take a walk and see some of the sights before we head back?" Marisa asks.

Her tone doesn't hold a hint of suggestion. Just two friends, talking while walking in the same direction. What am I going to say—no?

"Sure."

I ignore the paparazzi—probably hired by Claudette—and walk beside Marisa as we head toward the duomo.

"Here! Take my picture!" Marisa says, rushing ahead to pose by a fountain.

I pull out my phone and snap a few photos of her.

She beams. Poses seductively, dropping her coat off one shoulder and glancing at me. Her eyes smolder and she lets her lips part, trying to look sexy.

Why is this happening?

"Got some good ones," I call out, air dropping her the images.

She rolls her lips together and smiles. "Good! Those will be great for my socials next week." She bounds back to my side and wraps an arm around my back. "Say cheese for a selfie." She whips her phone out of her pocket.

Internally, I groan. Externally, I grin.

"Ready to head back? I'm getting cold," I say, putting my phone away.

Still no message from Nova. No phone call. Nothing.

The fact that I haven't heard from her all day is beginning to worry me. I know she's annoyed that I'm here; hell, I don't blame her. But it's not like her to ice me out on purpose. I mean, not for something we talked about and agreed on.

"Me too," she agrees. "I wish I could get a hot chocolate."

I give her a look. "The show's over."

She shrugs. "I have a photoshoot in two days."

"Is that why you had salad for dinner?"

"We can't all inhale plates of pasta to perform," she teases. Then, "I love my career. Brands put their trust in me when they make me the face of a campaign. Designers trust me when they invite me to walk in their shows. I won't let them down."

"I get that," I say. "I feel that way when I step onto the football field. Plus, what people—families—pay for tickets these days… I don't want to let anyone down."

"Exactly," Marisa agrees.

We set off in the direction of the hotel and relief begins to spark in my chest. I need to call Nova. I need to hear her voice.

When we're nearly in front of the entrance, Marisa slows and looks up at me. "Thank you for agreeing to my terms, West. I really appreciate you coming to Milan. Now that I know your situation, it couldn't have been easy to leave. But you attending the show will give the brand a nice bump in the press. I appreciate it."

"No problem," I say.

"And I'm happy for you that the Green Moose endorsement is working out. You'll be great for their line."

"Thanks."

She tugs on my arm, and I stop, glancing down to make sure she's okay.

She smiles. "Seriously, thank you."

I nod. "You're welcome."

Then, she grasps the front of my jacket and tugs, going up on her tippy toes. The way she's holding my coat catches me off guard. My hand automatically goes to her hip to keep her —and me—from stumbling.

Marisa presses a kiss to my cheek.

I freeze, unsure what the hell is happening. I jerk back just as she drops onto her toes.

"I've got to get my beauty sleep. I'll talk to you soon," she says.

Then, she waltzes through the entrance of the hotel. In the corner of my eye, I note the retreating back of a paparazzo.

Fuck! Did he photograph that?

"Marisa!" I hiss, storming after her.

But, for what? Kissing my cheek goodbye? Isn't that what friends do when they part ways?

Friends, maybe. But not two people who the world still suspects are in a fucking relationship!

The elevator doors close before I can question her. In fact, I don't think she notices I followed her inside.

Shit!

I feel the fight drain from my body as my heart rate accelerates and my nerves skitter. My ears ring and my head throbs.

I didn't do anything wrong. And still, my stomach is by my feet and my heart is in my temples.

I already know how those photos are going to look. The dinner, the laughter, the walk around Milan, the fucking embrace good night.

It's going to look like I screwed around with Marisa.

I need to get ahead of this.

Nova is going to see those photos.

Nova has no idea I had to go to dinner with Marisa.

I groan and head toward the bar. Sitting down, I order a vodka soda to clear my mind.

I call Nova. Then, I ring her again. Both times, I get her voicemail.

Me: Nova, please call me. We need to talk.

I move to call Callie when a text pops up.
My heart sinks when I note it's not from Nova.

Talon: (image of Marisa and West at dinner)

Talon: Heads-up, bro. Shit's about to go down with Nova.

Me: Fuck. Where'd you see that?

Talon: It's popping up online. You're tagged.

Avery: Don't answer any questions.

Me: What?

Cohen: You're about to get swarmed. There will be interest in your "relationship" with Marisa and how serious it's getting. Wear a hat at the airport tomorrow.

Talon: And a hoodie.

Avery: No comment. That's your answer to everything.

Cohen: Avery has experience with this—he knows.

Avery: Fuck off.

Cohen: Just saying.

Talon: Did you talk to Nova?

Me: Can't get in touch with her.

No one says anything and I take a gulp of my drink. The ice rattles in the glass as I take another swig.

Me: It's not like that.

Before I can explain further, my phone rings.
Again, it's not Nova, but I pick up in a hurry.
"Callie."
"What the hell, West?"
Shit. It's worse than I thought.

My phone skitters across the small table in the hospital waiting room.

Message after message. Image after image.

But I can't look at them. If I do, I'll break.

"I got here as soon as I could," Jacques announces, striding toward me.

I stand from my chair. Place my lukewarm coffee next to my jittery phone.

Jacques opens his arms and I fall into them.

"Shh, it's okay," he reassures me. "How is he?"

"He…collapsed." I squeeze my eyes shut as the image of Dad falling over in the kitchen replays in my mind.

I had just arrived at his house after a productive exchange with Pierre. He was at the stove, cooking a cassoulet for dinner. He turned when he heard me enter and the grin that cut across his face is seared into my memory.

He was so damn happy. Genuinely excited to see me. His eyes dropped from mine to my belly, as if clocking how much my little has grown. Then, he stepped toward the island. He gripped the edge and opened one arm for a hug. I went to him, wrapping my arms around his waist.

For a handful of heartbeats, I felt whole. Safe. Happy.

West was in Milan, finishing his obligations to Marisa Mella and her team. Pierre and I had cleared the air, and he was delighted for my happy news. And I was having dinner, at the vineyard, with Dad.

I pulled back and he beamed, lifting his glass of wine to take a swig. As I grabbed my phone from my bag to plug it into a charger, images started popping up.

"What the hell?" I muttered to myself, squinting at the screen.

I clicked on an image and felt my heart leap into my throat.

West. Marisa. Dinner.

Laughing. Touching. Drinking wine.

"What is this?" I whispered, clicking to the next image.

Marisa and West clinking wine glasses in cheers.

I choked back a gasp just as a loud clatter rang out behind me.

Turning, Dad was on the floor, a wooden spoon a few feet away.

"Daddy!" I yelled, running toward him.

He clutched his chest, his eyes wild, his breathing ragged.

Immediately, I called for an ambulance.

The minutes that ticked by before the arrival of the paramedics will haunt me for the rest of my life. The fear in his eyes is imprinted on my nerves. The tightness with which I clutched his fingers, tears streaming down my cheeks, wraps around my throat like vines.

I didn't know what to do. I didn't know how to react. I was fucking useless. No natural instincts.

Aren't mothers supposed to have those? Don't they just…know what the hell to do in an emergency? Instead, I froze. I panicked. I watched my dad falter and I shouted at him to…breathe. As if it was that fucking simple.

Oh, the relief that flooded my system when the paramedics arrived. The bustle of action—of people knowing what the hell to do —nearly made me weep. I rode with them to the hospital. I sat in the waiting room, desperate for news. They transferred him from our local hospital to Paris and I rode by his side. The entire time, my *stupid phone with the awful images was clasped in my hands, buzzing and ringing and beeping.*

"Nova," Jacques's voice is low.

"Hmm?" I shuffle back to look up at him.

I hate the concern and compassion in his eyes. "Sit down."

I plop back into my chair.

Jacques takes the seat next to mine and reaches for my hand. "Have you eaten?"

I frown. When was the last time I ate? As if in response to his question, a spell of dizziness makes me lightheaded. "I don't think so."

Jacques nods. "Where's Gabe?"

Oh, that's right. Gabe's here too. "He's getting food."

"Good. You need to eat, okay?" my brother reminds me gently.

My hand flies to my belly. To my little. I need to eat for him or her. Even if I'm not hungry. Even if the thought of food makes me nauseous. Fuck, how could I forget to eat? Aren't mothers supposed to intrinsically put their baby first? "I'll eat," I reply.

The pressure of Jacques's thumb on my fingers keeps me rooted to the moment. It stops me from mentally traveling back to the kitchen. To that handful of heartbeats I'll never get back. To the sound of Dad hitting the floor. A sickening thud. And that damn wooden spoon.

Shit. "Did I turn off the stove?"

"Everything at the house is fine," Jacques replies soothingly. "Here comes Gabe. Let's get you some food. The doctor will be out shortly with an update."

I frown at him. How does he know all that? He just got here. How does he have…information. Why is he so calm? Steady. Reliable.

"Breathe, Nov," Jacques whispers.

I suck in an inhale.

"Hey." Gabe's tone is also soft.

I frown at him. His eyes are wrecked when they hold mine.

"Is Dad—" I start.

Gabe shakes his head. "Dad's fine. They're going to have an update soon. He'll pull through, Nova." Gabe's eyes crinkle at the corners as he smiles softly. They remind me of Dad's eyes. "You've given him a good reason to stick around. Now, you gotta eat." Gabe unboxes a takeout container and places it on my lap. Then, he passes me a fork.

I jab at the salad and bring a few leaves to my mouth, munching on autopilot.

Gabe drops into the chair on my other side. The three of us are silent. Only the sounds of our breathing, our chewing, and the rustling of our takeout containers fills the air.

That and my stupid fucking phone.

"You okay?" Gabe asks. His eyes dart to my phone pointedly.

The girls have messaged. A constant stream of thoughts and questions in our group chat. I haven't responded to any of them. That's when they started calling. But, for obvious reasons, I haven't picked up either. I should let them know I'm okay. Physically at least. Mentally, I'm drained. Emotionally, I feel like I'm burning from the inside out. Like my entire existence is going up in flames and no one sees it.

"You saw the pictures?" I ask.

Gabe nods.

Jacques swears. "I can't believe he kissed her."

"What?" My neck snaps to his.

His eyes widen in horror.

"What the fu—" I start.

"Here." Gabe thrusts his phone at me.

I grab it and look at a new image. One where Marisa is holding the front of West's coat. Their heads are bent together, and her hair has fallen forward. But, from this angle, it's easy to tell that they're kissing.

They're fucking kissing!

The sentence blares in my mind like a foghorn and I shake my head to clear it.

Shit, I can't fall apart now. I need to be strong for Dad. For my little.

I pass Gabe his phone.

"I'm not okay," I admit. I haven't been okay—not really—in so fucking long. For a little bit—mere weeks—I thought I was thriving. I thought West and I were moving forward. I thought I was building a family with him.

What a silly, naïve girl I am.

Aren't moms supposed to know things? Like, have eyes in the backs of their heads or some shit? I didn't see this coming.

I believed West when he said his relationship with Marisa is a PR stunt.

But then, what the hell happened?

Because dinner and flirting and fucking kissing weren't part of the plan.

Those photos blindsided me.

And his messages…about how we need to talk. About what? His not-so-fake girlfriend? The truth is, I know nothing of his interactions with Marisa other than what he told me. But I saw the photos of them in New York City and Washington DC. I know she visited him in Knoxville. Was it more than he let on?

My thoughts spiral. My emotions are heightened. Everything I feel is sharp. Stabby. Fucking painful.

I was considering leaving my life here to support his career. To give up what I'm building so we can be together, all of us in the same place.

And then—where the hell would I be when West breaks my heart?

What would I have to show for myself? What lessons would I be teaching my child?

I clutch the fork hard enough to snap it.

"Eat," Jacques reprimands.

I take a bite of a salad I can't taste.

"You will be." Jacques's tone is laced with determination. Because he willed it, it must be so. "You will be okay, Nov."

He's always been like that, and I smile. Maybe Jacques is just the constant, steady, reliable sibling. Gabe's the charming, funny, ride or die. And I'm... God, right now I'm the fuckup.

I chew another bite.

"The family of Claude Martin," a doctor says.

My brothers and I stand. "We're his children," Jacques explains.

The doctor nods and hurries over, his expression unreadable.

"How is he?" Gabe asks.

The doctor lets out a long breath. "He's okay. Stable. There was another blockage and..." he continues but I don't hear any more words.

He's okay. Thank God.

I stagger on my feet. Jacques's arm bands around my waist to keep me from hitting the floor.

Dad's okay. He's stable.

Thank you. Thank you. Thank you.

I chant to the universe as a deluge of emotions sweeps through me.

The doctor leaves. Jacques walks me back to my chair.

"Breathe," Gabe says.

I pull in a breath.

"You're okay." My brother smiles. "And so is Dad."

Adrenaline leaves my body as relief flows through my limbs. Exhaustion like I've never known courses through me.

"I'll take her home," Gabe says, a thread of worry in his tone.

"Yeah. I think that's for the best," Jacques agrees.

They help me to my feet.

I stumble beside Gabe as he walks me to his car. The

second I'm buckled in, I drop my head to the cool pane of the window and close my eyes.

I vaguely remember Gabe carrying me into my flat. He orders me to change and gives me some privacy while I perform the necessary getting-ready-for-bed acts. Then, I collapse on my cozy mattress.

Gabe covers me with a duvet and turns off the light.

"You're okay, Nova," his voice follows me into sleep. "You've got this. All of it."

I wish I believed him.

WEST

She's sleeping when I enter the flat.

It's late. Too late. I should have been back hours ago, but my flight was delayed.

Sitting at the airport with a hat tugged low to conceal my identity, I stewed in silence. Nova didn't answer any of my calls. She didn't reply to any of my messages.

And worse? She hasn't been in contact with her friends either.

Fuck, I hurt her. I know she's icing me out and I don't blame her. But is she okay?

I reached out to Gabe and Jacques. Nothing.

I called the vineyard. No response.

The Martin family has closed ranks and while a part of me is happy that Nova has that type of support in her life, another part of me hates that they're protecting her from *me*.

Me! The man who loves her more than fucking life.

I take a seat in the chair in the corner of her bedroom that's usually piled high with clothes and watch her sleep. I clock the steady rise and fall of her chest. I note the slight part in her lips, the flutter of her eyelashes, the peaceful expression on her face. My beautiful girl. God, I love her.

And right now, she fucking hates me.

Nova shifts in her sleep, slowly waking up and stretching her arms overhead. Her eyes flutter open, and the sweetest, softest smile begins to cross her lips when she sees me.

I hang in that heartbeat—my entire being filling with her light.

And then, her eyes shudder closed and her mouth presses into a thin line. She remembers the night before. The photos. The gossip. The speculation. And hurt colors her irises.

It explodes in my stomach like a bomb, tiny shards of pain embedding throughout my body.

"You're here," she says, her tone accusatory.

"Nova." I stand from the chair and move closer to the bed.

She holds up a hand, warding me off. "No," she says, swinging her legs to the side of the bed and pushing to her feet. She reaches for her robe but not before I catch the soft swell of her belly. I don't know if my eyes are playing tricks on me or if it's the anguish of the moment, but her belly looks a tiny bit bigger than it did two days ago.

I already missed moments. And I'm about to miss so much more if I'm in fucking Knoxville and she's in Paris. Will she move to Tennessee? Does she want to raise our little together, under the same roof?

"We need to talk." My voice is quiet but firm. We needed to talk hours ago; now, I'm ready to jump out of my damn skin.

"My dad's in the hospital."

I rear back, replaying her words in my head to make sure I heard them correctly. "What?"

"Yesterday, he…collapsed. The ambulance came. They transferred him to a hospital in Paris because of his main surgeons; otherwise, I wouldn't even be here. I'd be at the vineyard."

"Is he okay?" I press, noting the emptiness in her tone. The…resignation.

She sighs. Shrugs. Her hands run over her stomach. "He's stable."

"Nova, I'm so sorry." I step toward her. She glares at me. "I had no idea."

Nova cocks her head to the side. "How was your date?"

Fuck. I shake my head. "It wasn't a date."

"Looked like one." She crosses her arms over her chest.

"Yeah," I agree.

Her eyebrows shoot up.

"I saw the pictures; I know what it looked like. But it wasn't a fucking date," I bite out. "I tried to call you. To give you a heads-up that—"

"That you were going out to dinner with Marisa Mella?" she supplies and when she says it, the truth sounds twisted. It sounds like a fucking cop-out.

I sigh. "It was a PR stunt. She added it once I got to Milan, and I didn't want to rock the boat. I just wanted to get it over with."

Nova snorts but hurt sweeps her expression. It blooms in her eyes and bleaches the color from her lips.

I feel it slam into my chest and it's followed by a wave of terror. Fuck.

"And the kiss?" she bites out.

I toss a hand in the air. "It wasn't a kiss!"

"She was holding on to your coat, gripping it. What? Did her hands and mouth and body all line up and perfectly land at the exact same second?" Nova's voice rises. "How stupid do you think I am, West?"

"What?" I stride toward her, my arm outstretched, my hand—

She slaps at it. "Don't touch me."

My hand falls to my side as terror begins to mount in my bloodstream. Little wisps of panic whisper fears I don't want to consider in the corners of my mind. "Nova, it was a PR stunt. It was dinner. And it's over. Marisa kissed my cheek good night at the end of the night. Like friends. That's it. I know the angle, and the press, and the social media shit is making it seem like more. But nothing happened. The contract is done. I got the endorsement. Marisa and I are—"

"You fulfilled the terms of your contract. You got your big deal. You did it, West." Nova slow claps, tears gathering in her eyes. Her voice is high and tight and laced with fucking heartache. "You're such a superstar," she tacks on, sarcasm dripping from every word.

"Nov." I grip the back of my neck, unsure what to do. What to say. Where the hell to put my fucking hands. I squeeze harder.

"And I'm supposed to—what? Give up my life here, follow you to Knoxville, and just hope things work out between us? What if they don't, West? What if we break up and I have no family and no career and no fucking identity other than being West Crawford's WAG?" her voice cracks. "Nothing about our situation has changed except that I've started building a life here, in Paris. And now, this happens." She throws a hand in the air. "How the hell am I supposed to react? What am I supposed to do?"

"Trust me!" I throw back, flailing my arms to the sides. "You're supposed to trust me, Nova. Because I've never given you a reason not to. What do you want from me? I have tried every way possible to prove myself to you. I showed up the second I heard you were pregnant, which, by the way, you didn't even have the decency to tell me. I've been at every appointment, read every damn book, and have spent my days trying to love you, trying to show you how much I fucking love you. I called you the second I learned about the dinner. I left you voicemails and messages. You never bothered to message me back."

"Don't you dare put this on me," Nova seethes. "My dad collapsed, West. Did you miss that part? Or does family not factor into things when—"

"Seriously?" I cut her off, my tone hard. My eyes narrow into slits. "You want to go there, Nova?"

She exhales, the color draining from her cheeks.

"Don't say something you can't come back from," I warn. "You know I'm worried about your dad. Your family is more family to me than my own."

"Fuck," she swears, rubbing at the center of her forehead. The fight leaves her as quickly as it built, and she sinks to the edge of the mattress. Red splotches of color linger on her cheeks but other than that, she looks drained. Disappointed eyes meet mine. She shakes her head. "I don't know where we go from here."

"What do you mean?" I ask softly, sitting beside her.

She shrugs one shoulder. "You have to go back to Tennessee this week anyway."

"Nova," my voice cracks. I reach for her hand and when she lets me hold it, I breathe a tiny exhale. "Nova, I want you to come with me, baby. I'm asking you to please consider moving to Tennessee. Not because I want you to give up what you're creating here. Not because I want you to be a WAG. But because, when the season starts, I can't be here. I want us to be in Knoxville together. As a family. And I will support anything—any dream—you have. You know I will."

"West," she breathes. Her sad eyes hold mine. She shakes her head. "I can't answer that right now. I'm—West, my dad is in the hospital. I'm still trying to process those photos. I'm…I'm so fucking angry. With you, with myself… And I'm hurt. I'm sad. I'm… I can't answer that right now."

As much as I appreciate her honesty and respect her for it, it's not what I want to hear.

"You have to go back to Knoxville this week," she repeats.

"It's a team meeting. I'll be back—"

"I think you should leave today," she cuts me off.

"What?" I shake my head. "No way. I'm not leaving until we sort this out. Talk to me, Nov."

"I...can't. I need to think. West..." Her tone is pleading. "Please, I need space right now. I need to show up for my dad. And you, being here, asking me to move, it's too much. And you were right, I don't want to say something I can't come back from. Please, just go to Knoxville. Do your team meeting. And we can talk next week."

Next week? "Nova," I say, my eyes holding hers. "You can't mean that."

"I do," she says, without an ounce of hesitation.

"Fuck. Nov, I didn't kiss her."

She rolls her lips together. "I believe you, West. But the fact that I questioned you at all...that's a problem, isn't it?"

"We're learning to trust each other again."

"Maybe," she says in that same resigned tone.

"I'm not leaving."

"But I'm asking you to," she pleads. "Please, give me the time and space I'm asking for. Respect me enough to let me think. To let me...breathe."

My stomach twists as her words gut me.

Anger jumps up next and I clench my fists, pressing to my feet to pace around her room. "That's what you really want? You want me to take off? So what? You can throw it in my face when—"

"I won't throw it in your face," she says so quietly, so earnestly, that I fucking believe her. "I just need some time alone."

"I can give you that while staying in Paris," I remind her.

"But you have to go back anyway. So go to the meeting. And then, we'll talk."

I snort. This is unbelievable. "You're not going to talk to me for the next three days? Seriously?"

She shrugs. "I'm asking you for space."

I let out an aggravated breath. "You know what? Maybe you're right. Maybe we could both use some space. Some fucking time. Because I don't know what else you want from me. I don't know how to prove to you that you're it for me. That I'm all fucking in, Nova. I've tried everything and it's still not enough. But I'm never enough, so no fucking surprise there, right?"

"West," she scolds me. "I didn't mean it like that."

"Didn't you?" I toss back.

Our eyes hold.

Anger and pain. So much fucking hurt.

Maybe this is how it will always be between us.

Maybe we'll just keep building each other up only to tear ourselves down.

"I'll call you," I tell her, gripping the suitcase I wheeled into the flat only a few hours earlier.

She doesn't reply.

I stride to the front door.

She doesn't follow.

I leave her flat, slide into a taxi, and head to the fucking airport, while booking a flight on my phone.

Nova doesn't call.

Hours pass as I wait for my flight to board. I drink a vodka soda. I wander around the airport. I fucking stew.

Reign: You good, man? A talked to Nova.

Me: Fine. Thanks for messaging.

Reign: We can...talk about it?

I snort. That must have been painful for him to ask. Still, I appreciate the concern.

Me: I'm straight. Thanks though.

I eat a pretzel and drink a Coke.
My phone beeps again.

Marisa: Hey! Thanks again for the support! I'm really happy with how the show was received. Your being there definitely boosted press coverage.

Marisa: How was your flight back? How's Nova? Did you ask her about the move yet?

Me: Glad to hear it. Congrats.

Me: Honestly? She's not talking to me.

Marisa: ???

Me: Those photos.

Marisa: Shit, are you serious?

Me: They look like we kissed.

Marisa: West! I'm so sorry! I had no idea we were even photographed after the duomo.

Me: Not your fault.

Marisa: It is!

I sigh. I don't want to play this fucking game. It is what it is, and Marisa apologizing doesn't change shit for me.

Marisa: I'm putting out a statement on Monday. Don't worry. I can fix this.

Me: There's nothing to fix. I mean, what's broken isn't your fault.

Marisa: Trust me, West. I got this.

Whatever. I slip my phone into my pocket.

Check my watch.

Heave out a sigh.

I miss Nova. As angry as I was a few hours ago, right now, I want to hold her in my arms and promise her that we'll make things work.

That I'm not giving up on us because I already know that I can't.

I'll never truly walk away from her. She's it for me. She and our little.

I glance around the airport. Travelers hurry to their gates. People loiter in the duty-free area, shopping.

And it hits me. What the fuck am I doing?

I didn't come to Paris to return to Knoxville empty-handed.

I'm all in.

It's Nova or nothing.

Hitching my backpack higher on my shoulder, I stride toward the exit.

Fuck this. I'm going home.

"You look good," I tell Dad as I lean forward in the chair beside his hospital bed. I take his hand, needing to know he's really okay.

He gives me some serious side-eye. "At least lie behind my back, Nova Jeanne."

I snort. "How are you feeling? Seriously?"

"Seriously," he sighs, closing his eyes for a beat. "I feel like I got hit by a truck."

I grip his hand tighter. He opens his eyes.

"But I'm good. Honestly. If you hadn't been there when I collapsed...well, I may not be here now. Thanks for saving my life, Nov."

I shake my head. "Don't go singing my praises. I was essentially useless."

Dad frowns. "Don't say that."

"Dad, I choked. Froze. Panicked."

"Ah, no," Dad moans, closing his eyes in pain.

"What is it?" I hunch closer.

"Stop admitting you're human. This whole time—years—I thought you were a mythical creature who—"

"Shut it!" I laugh, plopping down in my chair. "It's not funny."

"It's a little funny."

I sigh heavily, feeling some of my concerns dissipate. If Dad is joking around and being a pain in the ass, he's feeling better.

"Where's West?" Dad asks. "He should be back from Milan by now."

My mood sours instantly.

"Nova," Dad says quietly.

I roll my eyes. "We got in a fight."

"Because he had dinner with a supermodel after sitting front row at her fashion show," Dad summarizes.

"You know?"

He grins. "I know everything."

"Gabe showed you the photos."

"Instantly," Dad agrees. "I mean, I was getting live updates as news broke on social media."

"Jesus," I huff.

"Your brothers are pretty pissed off."

My eyebrows pull together. "What do you mean?"

"They like West. They were rooting for him. For this to happen…"

"I don't think he actually kissed her," I say, surprising myself for defending West.

"Me neither," Dad says easily.

I narrow my eyes.

"What?" he asks, holding up a hand. "You told me he was going to help her get some publicity so he could get an endorsement deal."

"Yeah. I didn't know he had to eat dinner with her."

"Okay." Dad shrugs. "I mean, dinner is hardly a scandal."

I frown. "You're supposed to be on my side." I gesture between us. "We share the same blood, remember?"

Dad chuckles. "How could I forget? I used to think I was a blood relative to a mystical being that—"

I groan, cutting him off.

"Nova, did you really look at the photos?"

"What? Yes, they're burned into my retina."

Dad smirks. "So, you noticed how stiff and uncomfortable West looks when Marisa kisses his cheek?"

I glare at Dad.

"Or the photo where it seems like he's going to stumble because she probably pulled his arm unexpectedly?"

I shake my head.

"No? Well, I noticed that," he says nonchalantly.

I swear softly and whip out my phone, pulling up the dreadful photos. Except, with a clear mind, I see what Dad's explaining.

West looks uncomfortable. Stiff and awkward. Uptight.

I sigh.

Dad smiles. "Maybe you should hear him out."

"Can't." I shake my head. "I told him to go to Knoxville. He left for the airport already."

Dad tries to sit up straight but I place a hand on his shoulder and shake my head.

"Why'd you do that?" His tone is accusing, and it almost makes me smile. He really does consider West to be part of our family.

"He has a meeting later this week." I shrug. "I need… time. Space. I need to…think."

"About what?" Dad lifts his eyebrows.

"Everything. I mean, what are we even doing? He's about to start the season and I'm working here and—"

"Do you love him?" Dad cuts me off.

"What?"

"Do you love him?" he repeats, slower this time.

"I—yes."

"Do you want to be with him?"

I nod.

"Do you trust him?" He narrows his eyes, searching my face as if to make sure I'm being honest.

Tears gather in the corners because...I do. Deep down, in my heart of hearts, I trust West Crawford more than I've ever trusted a man not related to me. But I fought it. Fought him.

Because... I'm fucking scared. Overwhelmed. And terrified of compromising all of me to support him.

Except...he's been here. Since the second he learned of my pregnancy, he's been here, in Paris. And he never asked me to compromise a damn thing.

"Yes," I answer on an exhale.

"So?" Dad tilts his head. "What are you still doing here?"

"Dad," I laugh. "I can't just—"

"Go to the airport and chase him down? Sure, you can. He'd do that for you," Dad says.

I stare at him. He stares back.

And then I stand and shoulder my purse. "Are you sure you'll be all right if—"

"Get out of here, Nova," Dad chuckles. "Also, Jacques told me you finished the tasting room."

"Yeah." I grin, proud of my work. "It's done."

"I can't wait to see it."

"I'll show you as soon as they spring you from here."

He grins. "And if you want to toss me the keys because an offer you can't refuse comes up in Tennessee, I'm in. I think doing wine tastings and chatting with customers could be good for me."

I stare at him, one tear slipping over and landing on my cheek. "I don't deserve you."

"You deserve the world." He says it like he means it. Like it's an obvious fact.

I chuckle, swiping my tear away. "All girls should have a dad like you."

He smiles. "Lucky for you, yours will."

I shake my head. "We don't know the sex of the baby."

Dad's smile widens. "It's a girl."

I roll my eyes.

"Go." He points to the door.

I bend over and kiss his cheek. "Love you, Daddy."

"Love you, Nov. Come back with good news."

I nod and stride toward the door.

Then, I race from the hospital, locate my car, and drive like mad to make it to the airport in time.

I don't even know what flight West is on.

I elect to valet my car at the airport terminal. With each passing minute, the desperation to make it in time, to see West, to fall into his arms, kiss his lips, and apologize, grows.

I'm half-panicked by the time I skid to a stop in front of the board showing all the departing and arriving planes.

And the flight to Knoxville departed nine minutes ago.

"Shit," I swear, rubbing at the center of my forehead. I'm too late.

The panic seeps out of me as disappointment takes its place.

I missed him.

I pull out my phone to send him a text but...what's the point? He won't be able to read it until the plane lands.

Sighing, I debate if I should buy a ticket and fly after him. But I don't have a suitcase. Or my passport.

Shaking my head, I walk back to the valet stand to retrieve my car.

Then, I slide inside and drive toward my flat, my tears drying on my cheeks by the time I get there.

I'm parking my car when my phone rings with a phone number I don't recognize.

I debate letting it go to voicemail but—what if it's connected to West?

"Hello?" I answer.

"Hi, is this Nova?" a woman's voice asks.

I clear my throat. "Yes. Who's calling please?"

"Nova, hi! It's Marisa Mella."

My mouth drops open, and I clutch the phone tighter. "Hi," I say lamely, unsure what to say. Why is she even calling?

"I just wanted to let you know that West talked about you and your baby the entire time we had dinner together. I had no idea that he was in a serious relationship or that you were expecting when I asked him to come to the fashion show. And the photos that were published? Well, they look like West and I were on a date and then, I kissed him. But we really just had dinner, talked about you guys and how much he wants you to move to Knoxville, and took a walk. Then, I thanked him for his support, kissed his cheek goodbye, and that was it."

I close my eyes as my heart rate accelerates. She doesn't tell me anything I don't know. And while I appreciate her calling, I don't need her confirmation because West already gave me his word. I believe him. That was never our problem. It was more about trusting myself than it was about trusting his intentions.

"I was just coming to that realization," I reply. "West is a great guy, and he wouldn't lie about something when he could just be honest."

"West is fantastic but from what I hear, so are you. I'm really happy for you both. I'm sure you're overwhelmed navigating everything, but I wanted to clarify things—your man loves you. And he wouldn't do anything to jeopardize that."

"Thank you. Thanks for…calling."

"No problem. Take care of yourself. Hope our paths cross one day. I heard you want to be a fashion designer."

I straighten in my seat. West told her *that*? Jesus, he really must have talked about me for most of dinner. "It's just a dream…"

"If you want it, keep after it. And if there's anything I can help with, please reach out."

Gah. Why does she have to be so…genuinely kind?

"Thank you. Truly, I appreciate your reaching out."

"Have a good night, Nova."

"You too." I end the call.

I slip my phone into my purse and spend a few minutes just sitting in my car.

Wishing that West was here.

That when I walk into the flat, he'll grin at me over his shoulder and tell me what he whipped up for dinner.

That we'll share details about our day, laugh over a home-cooked meal, and cuddle beneath a blanket while watching a movie.

God, I miss him.

And this time, I have no one to blame but myself.

25

WEST

I turn a page in the baby book, my eyes skimming over the questions and spaces for parents to write in their response.

What are the headlines on the day of baby's birth?

This is what baby wore home from the hospital! (Place photo here)

Baby's first word?

Baby's first steps?

I skim my fingertips across the page.

Did my mom care about any of those milestones? Did anyone?

It hits me how different my baby's childhood will be. How much love will surround him or her as they grow their first tooth and take their first steps.

I lean back in the rocking chair as the key turns in the front lock.

I pause, listening as Nova enters the flat.

My eyes drop closed as I listen to her moving around the space. Setting down her purse. Shrugging out of her coat. Taking off her boots.

The normal sounds of ordinary that I never take for granted. Probably because they're the sounds of safety and stability. Of home.

I smile to myself.

I move to push to my feet and let Nova know that I'm here when a knock sounds on the front door.

I lean back in the rocking chair. Who could that be?

Her brothers? A friend?

"Pierre!" Nova exclaims, her tone surprised.

Fucking Pierre. What the hell does he want?

"Nova," the Frenchman says. "Is this a bad time?"

"No, not at all. Would you like to come in?" The door creaks as she pulls it wider.

"That's all right," he says.

Good man. I begin to change my tune where he's concerned.

"I just wanted to drop off a little gift for you and the baby. I was so happy when you shared the news the other day."

"Thank you," Nova replies. The crinkle of tissue paper floats through the air. "And thank you again for lunch."

Lunch? When the fuck did they have lunch?

Jealousy crawls up my throat, but I swallow it back. As if I have a leg to stand on in this moment. I glance around the nursery and sigh.

"After going through the numbers with you, I came to a decision. I wanted to tell you in person."

"What's this?" Nova asks.

"Open it," Pierre replies.

The silence that follows causes my annoyance to heighten. What the hell did he give her? Another gift? Why?

"Oh, Pierre! Seriously?" Nova asks.

"Yes. We'd love to start distributing Martin wines in Le liège."

The third restaurant.

"This is wonderful news. Thank you." Nova sounds truly happy.

I let out a sigh of relief. It's a contract. A business opportunity.

"Thank you, Nova. I'm thrilled our partnership is expanding."

"So am I."

"Well, I better be going."

"You can come in," she offers again.

Why? Let him go!

"Another time," he says.

There will be no other times.

"I have, well, I have a date," he continues.

Good!

"Oh, that's great, Pierre. Have a good night," Nova says, sounding happy for him.

Relief flickers through my limbs and I let out a breath I didn't realize I was holding.

"*Bonsoir*," he replies.

The door snicks closed.

I hear the gas stove light and imagine Nova is heating water for a cup of tea.

I stand and move to the doorframe. Then, I take a deep breath and step into the kitchen.

"Nov—"

"Argh!" she screams, her hand flying to her chest.

"Sorry!" I exclaim, holding up my hands. "I didn't mean to scare you."

"Creeping out of my baby's nursery while I'm alone in the flat? What the fuck did you think would happen?" she snaps back.

Our eyes hold for a heartbeat. Then another.

And then, we both begin to laugh.

Nova bends forward, her hands gripping her knees, as her blonde hair falls forward and her body shakes with laughter.

I'm practically crying, pinching the bridge of my nose to get a freaking grip as I cackle.

She straightens and grips her side. Shaking her head, she says, "I went to the airport. Your flight had left."

She went to the airport? I grin. "I didn't get on it."

"Why?" Her eyes spark with challenge.

"Because I wanted to come home."

Nova frowns. "Knoxville is—"

"You're my home, Nova. You and our little. I said I'm not going back to Knoxville without you, and I meant it."

"But you have a team meeting."

I shrug. "I'll either make it or I'll accept the fine. But you're the most important person in my life. And I'm not going anywhere until I know we're okay. I respect you more than anyone but I'm not giving you time or space. Not for this. I'm giving you me. You wanna fight? Let's fight. You wanna cry? I'll hold you. You wanna get a jab in? Right here." I tap the right side of my jaw.

Nova snorts. Then she heaves out a sigh and stares at me. "What if I want to kiss and make up?"

I smile. "Best fucking idea I ever heard." I laugh. "But I don't believe you. I know I hurt you and—"

"Marisa called."

Surprise causes my eyebrows to lift. "She did?"

"Yeah. She explained everything. But I had already come to the same conclusion after talking to Dad. I know you didn't kiss her. And I do trust you, West. More than anyone. I'm just… I'm scared."

"Of what?" I ask, leaning back against the counter and crossing my arms over my chest.

"Losing myself," she sighs, her palm resting against her stomach. "I can't wait to be a mother. Truly. But I worked hard to get the tasting room the way I want it. I started to carve out a life here, in Paris. I don't want to follow you to Knoxville and…just be West Crawford's baby mama."

I laugh but cut it off when I note that she's serious.

"You could never just be West Crawford's anything when you're a million times more than anything I'll ever be." I step closer. "Nova, I will never try to change you. I will always support your dreams. Whatever they are, I'm in. I'm always on your side. But I don't want to live in two different countries. I don't want to co-parent. I want you. I want our little. I want our family. Together. All the fucking time. Forever."

She nods, a smile spreading across her face. "I do, too."

I open my arms and she falls into them. I hold her close, letting the feel of her heartbeat, even and steady, soothe me. "I hate that it took talking to your dad and Marisa to convince you, Nova."

"I would have gotten to the right answer eventually, West. Just like you said, we'd have found our way back to each other. I think that will always be true."

I sigh heavily. "I can't lose you, Nova Jeanne. I won't."

"You won't," she confirms. "But West..." She pulls back to look at me.

"Yeah?"

"You have to go to this team meeting. You made a commitment. And I can't come this week."

I bite my cheek to keep from laughing. I love how literally she took my words because...I meant them literally. "Why not?"

"I'm taking my dad to see the tasting room. I promised as soon as he's out of the hospital. I'm...well, I'm going to turn the reins over to him and hope he doesn't fuck it up."

We both laugh because Claude Martin doesn't do fuckups.

"You did an incredible job with your family's business. Designed the tasting room and closed one of the biggest accounts," I remind her.

"Yeah," she breathes out. "I guess my work here is done."

I tilt my hips forward so she can feel how badly I want her. "Or just getting started."

She snorts at my lame joke. Then, her eyes turn serious. "Can you kiss me now?"

I nod, lowering my face to hers. "But I'm not going to stop."

"Promise?" she whispers, her eyes dropping to my mouth.

"Swear it." Then, I press my lips to hers and kiss her slowly.

Thoroughly.

Passionately.

I make love to Nova Jeanne Martin until I forget where I end, and she begins. And I don't want to come up for air.

Not ever.

"It's official," I say, showing West my phone.

His eyes scan the screen as he reads aloud, "Marisa Mella tells fans that she and West Crawford ended their brief relationship months ago but remained good friends. She explains that's why he came to cheer her on and catch up over dinner when she walked in the Hansen Cross Fashion show in Milan last weekend. 'It's always great to catch up with West! He's a great guy and I wish him all the luck and success,' Marisa told *The Best Beat*. So, that puts rumors to rest. Kind of. Because it seems Marisa has been stepping out with The Burnt Clovers' bass player, Jameson Tate, who is off-again with long-time girlfriend Amelia—'" West stops reading and looks at me.

I shrug. "Allegra says they had dinner."

"Wow! Damn, that would be great for Jameson," West says, moving back to the kitchen island and picking up his coffee mug. "He and Marisa would better understand each other's schedules and commitments. They'd be more supportive of each other."

I smile. "Maybe." I shake my head. "Who knew we'd end up with Marisa Mella as a friend?"

West chuckles. "Or that she'd be dating Jameson."

"Allegedly."

"Allegedly," he agrees.

"So…"

"So?" West asks.

I grin. "In the next few weeks, we can share our news. Publicly." I glance down. "My bump is getting harder and harder to hide."

"You're barely showing."

I snort and give him a look.

He shrugs. "I think you look sexy as fuck."

"That's because you put a baby in me," I remind him. "It's probably some biological response that you're going to be attracted to me because I'm growing your kid. But afterwards—"

"I'll always be attracted to you." He smacks my ass.

I roll my eyes. "Yeah. Yeah."

A wicked gleam comes into West's eyes. "Want me to show you?"

"Now?" I gasp, glancing at the clock.

"You're hilarious! You feign shock but I see you clocking the time." He steps closer. "We have time, Nova."

"We're meeting my dad, brothers, and Haley—"

"In an hour," West says, placing a hand on my hip. "Trust me, we won't be late. Your brothers are just starting to like me again."

I snort, knowing West committed to a shopping afternoon with Gabe as well as a round of golf with Jacques to get into their good graces again. I bite my bottom lip and look up. "I still have to shower."

"Okay." He drops his mouth to my neck and presses a kiss to the sensitive space where my neck meets my shoulder. His hand slides around to my ass and he grabs a handful.

"And dry my hair."

"Uh-huh," he agrees, nipping at my earlobe.

I sigh, my hands gripping his ass and pulling him closer. I

feel his hard length press into my stomach, and I melt into him.

"There's makeup," I mutter to no one.

West takes my chin and angles my face. He smiles as he presses a kiss to the tip of my nose. And then, his mouth is on mine, and I stop caring about my hair and makeup and dinner.

Instead, I wrap my arms around West's shoulders. He pulls me into his frame and deepens our kiss. Making sure he doesn't squish my bump, he turns me around so I'm facing the kitchen counter. Then, he trails kisses down my neck, as his hands push my leggings off my hips.

"Here?" I pant, glancing around the kitchen.

"Why not?" he replies, tapping my ankle until I lift my foot and he can peel off my leggings. Then, he removes them from the other leg. His hands skate up the backs of my legs and I nearly shudder from the view he must have.

My guy works fast because he pulled my panties off with my leggings. The cold air hits my exposed flesh as West kneads the tops of my thighs.

"West," I mutter.

"Hm?" He remains on his knees as his palm slides over my ass cheek before curling around to clutch my hip. Then, he drags his tongue over my pussy, and I cry out.

My hands fly to the island, and I grip the edge as West spreads my ass cheeks. His tongue makes long, deep passes, as his hands grip at my ass.

Instantly, my breasts grow heavier. I brace my arms as he buries his face and begins to eat me out from behind. He moans and smacks his lips as I widen my stance, practically grinding against his face because it feels so fucking good.

"Turn around, baby," he demands.

I do, spinning so the island cuts into my back. I brace my hands on the cool surface, my fingers hooking around the edge as West raises one of my legs and tosses it over his shoulder.

Jesus, seeing him on his knees before me, worshipping my body, is nearly enough to make me come.

He licks me again, slow and deep, before adding pressure from his fingers as he plays with my clit. Small, even circles, that spread my arousal and have me breathing harder.

West looks up at me and winks. "I wish you could see my view, baby. It's fucking breathtaking."

I shudder from the desire in his tone. He begins to lick and suck on my clit as two fingers slowly pump into me.

It's a steady rhythm that has me climbing a peak I want to fling myself off of.

"Oh, God. West," I pant.

He increases the pace. The pressure. The fucking friction.

He turns his head and drags his nose along my inner thigh, nipping at my skin.

My knees nearly give out and my knuckles turn white from how hard I'm gripping the countertop. Then, West slows his pace. With deep tongue thrusts and lazy circles, he plays with my pussy like we have all day. Like there's nothing else he'd rather be doing.

And—fuck—I think that's the truth.

His steadiness, the trust I have in him to take care of me, brings me to the precipice. My thighs begin to shake but West never changes his pace.

"West," I beg.

"Come for me, baby," he murmurs, pressing on my clit. "Shatter on my tongue and let me taste how fucking sweet you are."

His words send me over the edge, and I cry out, arching my back, as I come apart on his face. He continues to lap and lick, moaning as my want coats his tongue.

When the orgasm recedes, West stands and pulls me into his arms. My knees feel weak and I clutch at his shoulders.

He kisses me deeply, pushing his tongue into my mouth so I can taste myself. I reach for him, my hand palming his shaft through the thick denim of his jeans.

"Did licking me turn you on?" I murmur. He's so fucking hard. His cock twitches against my palm.

"Always does," he mutters.

I grin. He curls my hair behind my ears and cups my face as he looks at me. Then, he kisses me soulfully. I lose myself in his kiss as I work his jeans and boxers off his hips.

West grips the back of his shirt and whips it off before he focuses on the tiny buttons of my sweater. His fingers are surprisingly nimble as he opens the row.

My breasts fall free, and he sighs, testing the weight of my right breast before tweaking my nipple. "No bra?"

I laugh. "I was hoping we'd end up here."

"Fucking in the kitchen?"

"Actually." I glance over my shoulder. "Can we relocate to the living room for the next part? The kitchen isn't exactly comfortable, and my knees aren't meant for the cold tiles."

West smirks. "Baby, I gotta tell you something. It's probably not the right time, and I don't want to hurt your feelings but…"

"What?" I press.

"Your living room isn't much better. That's gotta be the most uncomfortable fucking couch I've ever sat on. In my life."

I sputter a laugh and shake my head. Still, I tug on his hand and relocate him to the living room. Pushing on his shoulder, I make him sit on the couch he hates.

"Will you like it more if I fuck you on it?" I offer.

"It could help change my opinion," he agrees.

I smile. He grins.

Then, I push West back against the cushions and shimmy closer. "Don't think about the spring in your back—"

He laughs.

I take his hands and place them on my bare breasts. "Focus on me."

His laughter dies and his eyes meet mine. Darken. Hold.

I straddle his thighs and sink down on his hard cock, one inch at a time. When I reach the root, he thrusts upward slightly, making sure we're completely fused. His hands play with my breasts as I grab the back of the couch and begin to set a pace. I grind on him as his one hand drops to my belly. He pulls my nipple into his mouth, and I cry out, pushing out my chest, as I work him over faster.

"Fuck, beautiful," he swears, releasing my breast and letting his head drop back.

His hands grip my hips as I move faster, gliding up and down on his hard length.

His fingers dig into my flesh as he pants. I drop my head back and the ends of my hair tickle my back as I find a rhythm that has us both crying out.

"Look at me, Nova," West demands.

I force my eyes open and meet his gaze.

His eyes are darker than midnight. A severe expression cuts across his face. He holds my gaze, never blinking, as he demands, "Come for me. Come again, baby. Break apart and give it to me."

"Oh, God," I groan.

West pushes up into me, meeting me thrust for thrust. On the third time, I shatter. I grasp my own breasts as I scream his name.

"Good girl," he pants, rocking into me once. Then, twice. And then, "Fuck, Nova Jeanne." He comes on a roar.

I feel him let go. His hot cum leaks down my inner thighs. I sigh and collapse against West as he hugs me to him. My forehead falls to his shoulder as I try to regulate my breathing.

When I'm able to straighten, West tips his face up to kiss me hard. "I love you, baby."

"Love you more, West."

His hand cups my abdomen and he places another kiss on my shoulder.

I let out a shaky exhale. "I could stay here with you all day but...I really do need to shower."

He chuckles. "And dry your hair. I know." With that, he holds me tight and pushes to his feet, walking us both to the shower.

"We can't be late to our own goodbye dinner," I say reasonably as West turns on the showerhead and tests the water.

"That's fair," he agrees. Then, he nods at me. "It's hot enough."

"Thanks." I step into the shower.

West follows me inside.

We shower together, talking and laughing, our movements unhurried.

Like we have all the time in the world.

I guess it's because...we do.

And it's the best feeling ever.

We're ten minutes late to meet my family for dinner at Le liège.

"Don't." Jacques holds up a hand when he sees my face. "I don't want to hear any bogus reasons for why you're late."

Haley blushes as Gabe cackles.

West snorts before turning to hug my dad hello.

I give Jacques the middle finger which he swiftly returns. "So ladylike," my brother teases me.

We sit down at the table and Pierre sends over a bottle of celebratory champagne.

West stands to thank him and as I watch my man

exchange pleasant words with Pierre, I know that we truly are moving forward. Both of us, together.

"To your next chapter," Dad says, raising his glass.

"To your next chapter," I counter.

Dad laughs. "I'll be great at the tasting room."

"You're always great," I reply.

"Jesus," Gabe mutters. "Can you tell who the favorite child is?" He looks at West.

West bites back his laughter.

"Cheers!" Haley calls out.

"*Santé!*" Jacques agrees.

Dad and I chuckle as we all cheers and take sips of our drinks. A non-alcoholic sparkling wine for me and champagne for everyone else.

"You ready for what's next?" I murmur to West.

He turns toward me and smiles. "With you?"

I nod.

"Always."

"Jesus, you'd think it wouldn't be this bad since she's already knocked up," Gabe mutters accusingly.

We all laugh, but underneath the table, West reaches for my hand.

I lace our fingers together and squeeze.

He squeezes back twice.

Always.

EPILOGUE

WEST

Nova shared her dad's prediction with me, and it turns out, Claude Martin is correct.

Stella Kent Crawford is born on her due date, November 3. She immediately lives up to her name, entering the world with the brightness of a star and fulfilling every wish I never knew I had. Those first few weeks are a transition as I try to balance football with having a newborn baby.

But, no surprise, Nova is a natural. She wakes every time Stella whimpers. She spends early mornings singing lullabies in French and walking around the nursery I created in our condo in Knoxville.

While I've missed Stella's first smile (I was playing a game in New York) and her first fever (I was beside myself, rushing home from a game in Dallas), I try to spend every second I can with my baby girl.

Hell, with both of my girls.

And today is a special first I'm stoked to capture.

Stella is one month old and coming to her first football game to watch Daddy play.

"Man, keep your eyes on the goddamn field," Avery lectures.

Cohen snorts, "He can't help himself."

"Yeah," my teammate Leo adds. "His girls are here."

I glance up quickly to note where Nova and Stella are sitting in the family suite. I hope they're comfortable. I hope Stella's warm enough. Did Nova pack an extra blanket? And her little pink giraffe that Uncle Gabe sent?

"Crawford!" Avery growls.

I nod and get my head back in the game. I want to make my girls proud.

Forcing myself to acknowledge that Nova and Stella are perfectly fine, I focus on football. When Avery calls the next play, I grin. I fucking got this.

Avery accepts the snap and I take off, running down the field and cutting wide to get open.

I turn to see the football spiraling perfectly just where I want it to. Running faster, I push myself to my capacity, my lungs burning, my legs pumping, just as the ball falls into my hands. I cradle it to my chest and sprint into the endzone, avoiding the defenders who try to take me down.

Touchdown! I toss my hands in the air and point at my baby girl.

Nova catches my eyes, screaming for me, a wide smile on her face.

Damn, she's fucking beautiful.

"Way to go, Crawford!" Cohen hollers.

Talon comes on the field and makes the extra point.

We play hard for the rest of the quarter and when the clock runs out, the Coyotes win 24-16.

"Stella's your good luck charm," Leo tells me as we relocate to the lockers.

"Sure is," I agree. I shower as quickly as I can, desperate to see my baby.

When I exit the locker room, Nova and Stella are waiting.

"Nice game, West," Raia calls out. I nod my thanks as I beeline to Nova.

"You were amazing!" Nova exclaims, glancing at our sleeping daughter. "Wasn't Daddy incredible?" she whispers.

"Come here." I wrap an arm around Nova's back and pull her and Stella into my embrace. I kiss Nova hard before placing the gentlest kiss on sweet Stella's forehead. "How long did she sleep?"

"She caught your touchdown," Nova replies.

I roll my eyes and Nova laughs.

"She was out for most of the game."

"Was she warm enough?" I worry.

"She was," Nova promises.

We exchange a smile.

"Thanks for bringing her today," I say, meaning it. Everything about this game felt different. More important. And I know it's because Stella was in the stands. God, I hope I make her proud.

"I'm sure this is just the beginning of her being at all your games!" Nova laughs.

"Hope so," I agree, taking Stella from Nova's arms to give her a cuddle before I place her in the bassinet of her stroller. "Ready to go home?"

"Don't you want to"—Nova gestures toward the team—"go celebrate at Corks?"

I shake my head. "Not today. I want to go home and celebrate with you."

Nova chuckles. "She's not going to sleep *that* long."

I grin. "We can order takeout and watch a movie."

Nova bites her bottom lip. "And talk about Christmas plans?"

I lift an eyebrow. "Sure. What do you have in mind?"

"Well," she sighs. "My entire family wants to come."

I grin. "Hell yeah! I was hoping they'd come for Stella's first Christmas. Are you sure you don't want to go to Paris?" I ask as I begin to stroll Stella toward the exit.

She shakes her head. "No. You have a home game that

week. We'll all come watch you play. Be together for Christmas morning."

"Sounds perfect," I say, meaning it. Nova's family has truly welcomed me with open arms, giving me the stability and love that I've missed out on for most of my life. It makes me so happy to know that my daughter will never not have that.

We reach Nova's SUV and I transfer Stella from her bassinet to the car seat, double-checking that everything is secure.

"By the way," Nova says as I close the car door. "Marisa is in town next week and I invited her over for dinner."

"Mella?" I ask.

She nods. Bites that bottom lip again.

"Okay. Is she coming?" I ask.

Nova grins. "Yeah, she's coming. But also, I'm going to run some ideas by her."

My eyes widen and excitement thrums through my veins. "Still dreaming about that fashion line?"

Nova glances through the window at Stella. "Yep. But a baby line."

"A baby line," I repeat.

"Marisa thinks it has potential."

"You've already spoken about it?"

Nova shrugs. "Just sent her some preliminary sketches but…yeah."

"Good. Nova." I tug her closer and drop a kiss to the crown of her head. "You should do it! It will be incredible."

"Marisa is a great resource," she says slowly. "And…"

"And?"

"She's bringing Jameson!"

"Seriously?" I laugh. "Are they really dating?"

"Seems like it. We'll get the tea next week."

I laugh and brush a kiss across her lips.

"Okay, I'll follow you home and then we'll get takeout from Alberto's."

"Mm," Nova agrees. "Tacos would hit the spot."

"I'll hit that spot," I remind her.

She laughs, squeezing my hand. "I know you will."

I squeeze back twice. "Tonight."

"As long as you don't fall asleep," she calls over her shoulder, moving to the driver's door.

"That happened once!" I defend myself. It was after a tough loss and a late flight and instead of giving it to Nova, I passed out. To this day, it bothers me.

Nova's laugh, pure music, rings out. "I'll see you at home."

"I'll be right behind you, baby."

She gives a little wave and slides into the SUV.

She waits for me to get into my ride—a sensible Porsche Cayenne since I'm a dad now—before she pulls out of the parking lot.

We go home together. Just the way I wished it.

And it's better than anything I ever imagined.

Because deep down, I know it's for always.

Thank you so much for reading Surprised and Sacked! Don't miss more Knoxville Coyotes Football coming soon! Preorder Trapped and Tackled now!

ACKNOWLEDGMENTS

All of my heartfelt thanks to Amy Parsons, Becca Mysoor, Erica Russikoff, Ann Jones, Virginia Carey, Amber, Sheila Dohmann, Melissa Panio-Peterson, Kate Farlow at Y'all. That Graphic, Dani Sanchez and the Wildfire Marketing Solutions team. I value your insight and support infinitely.

Many thanks to the cover model Justin and photographer Stephanie – it was wonderful to work with you both!

A big shoutout to the Castle Crew — y'all are the best and I'm so thankful for your friendship.

So much love to the book bloggers, bookstagrammers, booktokkers, and book lovers! Thank you for taking a chance on my words and reading Knoxville Coyotes Football!

To Tony and our littles — you're my whole world. I love you.

ALSO BY GINA AZZI

Knoxville Coyotes Football:

Faked and Fumbled

Surprised and Sacked

Trapped and Tackled

The Burnt Clovers Trilogy:

Rebellious Rockstar

Resentful Rockstar

Restless Rockstar

Tennessee Thunderbolts:

Hot Shot's Mistake

Brawler's Weakness

Rookie's Regret

Playboy's Reward

Hero's Risk

Bad Boy's Downfall

Boston Hawks Hockey:

The Sweet Talker

The Risk Taker

The Faker

The Rule Maker

The Defender

The Heart Chaser

The Trailblazer

The Hustler

The Score Keeper

Second Chance Chicago Series:

Broken Lies

Twisted Truths

Saving My Soul

Healing My Heart

The Kane Brothers Series:

Rescuing Broken (Jax's Story)

Recovering Beauty (Carter's Story)

Reclaiming Brave (Denver's Story)

My Christmas Wish

(A Kane Family Christmas

+ *One Last Chance* FREE prequel)

Finding Love in Scotland Series:

My Christmas Wish

(A Kane Family Christmas

+ *One Last Chance* FREE prequel)

One Last Chance (Daisy and Finn)

This Time Around (Aaron and Everly)

One Great Love

The College Pact Series:

The Last First Game (Lila's Story)

Kiss Me Goodnight in Rome (Mia's Story)

All the While (Maura's Story)

Me + You (Emma's Story)

Standalone

Corner of Ocean and Bay

ABOUT THE AUTHOR

Gina Azzi writes Contemporary and Sports Romance with relatable, genuine characters experiencing real life, love, friendships, and challenges. Dive into her sports romance series: Knoxville Coyotes Football, Boston Hawks Hockey, and Tennessee Thunderbolts, or get lost in her rockstar romances in The Burnt Clovers trilogy.

A Jersey girl at heart, Gina has spent her twenties traveling the world, living and working abroad, before settling down in Ontario, Canada with her husband and three children. She's a voracious reader, daydreamer, and coffee enthusiast who loves meeting new people.

Connect with her on social media or through www.ginaazzi.com.